THINKING ABOUT YOU

THINKING ABOUT YOU

MONICA MURPHY

Cover design: Hang Le
byhangle.com

ONE

CANNON

I'M SURROUNDED by hundreds of uppity British people. Just listening to their heavily accented voices is making me feel stupid. Like some of them I can't even understand. And then there's the fact that most of them are looking at me like I'm some sort of alien from another planet.

I can't help it if I'm twice their size. Besides, most of them look really skinny. Downright frail.

"I feel like a dumbass," I mutter, shaking my head.

My close friend and teammate Jordan Tuttle—who's standing right next to me—laughs. "Why do you say that?"

It's Saturday night and we're in London, at a welcoming party for our team held at a fancy restaurant. We play for the San Francisco 49ers and we're in an exhibition game tomorrow at Wembley Stadium, which is some dream-come-true type shit right there. A social group—I don't remember the name, but it's led by a dude who I think is a duke or whatever—decided to throw us a party in celebration of tomorrow's game.

I came for the free food and booze. Oh, and because we had to show up and put in a good appearance for the team.

But the food isn't that great—a bunch of crappy appetizers that don't look particularly appetizing and taste like nothing. The only booze available is white wine, while I'm more of a beer drinker or a shot taker.

"I don't fit in here," I say to Tuttle, our quarterback, though he's not really paying attention to me. No, he's watching his girl Amanda, who flew to London to be with him this weekend, and who is currently standing on the other side of the room. They were a couple in high school during our senior year—we all went to the same school, so I know Amanda pretty well. Now they're trying to get back together and I'm all for it.

I'm even a little jealous of it.

"None of us fit in here," Tuttle says, never taking his gaze off Amanda. "We're all Americans."

"Yeah, but you got this high society shit down," I tell him. He sends me a questioning look, and I continue, "It's true. Your rich family is all high and mighty. You've got manners and shit."

I may have money now, but I will *never* have Tuttle's wealth or background.

He actually snorts. "We're not high and mighty. Don't forget my dad is a complete asshole."

"Who makes a lot of money, and that makes him high and mighty," I remind him.

"Just because someone is worth a lot of money doesn't mean they have class." Tuttle finally glances over at me. "And you make a lot of money, so doesn't that make you high and mighty by your definition?"

Sometimes I hate that Tuttle is too smart for my own good. The guy is constantly showing me up. Not that it's difficult —he's definitely smarter than me. He always has been, and I've accepted that fact.

"Fine, whatever." I wave a hand and take a step closer to him, lowering my voice. "It's different over here. These people, you just look at them and you can tell they're all a bunch of snobs."

"You really think so?" Jordan's voice is full of doubt.

"Oh, I know so. I mean, listen to them." I raise my voice, giving it a shrill edge, trying to imitate one of the women I overheard earlier. "Oh my, just look at those American football players! They're so disgustingly large and—quite beastly.'" I roll my eyes. "I heard a lady actually say that a few minutes ago."

"Beastly?" Tuttle raises an eyebrow. "I kind of like it."

"You shouldn't." I am broad. And I can be menacing, especially out on the field. I know this. But beastly? "It's a total insult."

"Hmm, I'm not so sure about that. I happen to quite like beastly men," says a sweet, soft voice from behind me.

Oh. Shit.

Panic freezes me, my gaze meeting Tuttle's. His eyebrows are so far up they're practically in his hairline, and his lips are curved into a smirk. The look on his face says *busted*.

The feeling in my gut says *busted* too.

Clearing my throat, I slowly turn, pasting on a smile that immediately fades once I lock eyes on the petite woman standing in front of me. Our gazes meet, her eyes bright and full of mischief, and I'm immediately assailed with a multitude of things, all of them coming at me at a rapid-fire pace. Here's what I can remember.

She's blonde.

Blue-eyed.

Pink cheeked.

And she's smiling at me.

Oh, and her teeth are fucking perfect.

"H-hi." The word stumbles out of me, confirming that yep, I am a total dumbass, just like I thought. I clear my throat once more and try again. "Hello."

My voice is smooth and even. Huge improvement.

Her smile grows. "Hello."

Tuttle elbows me in the back, shoving me toward her, and I practically fall over. "I have a question."

"Yes?" She sounds amused, and her eyes are twinkling. Her dark blonde hair is sleek and falls past her shoulders, and she's wearing a blue dress that brings out the color of her eyes. Her cheeks are prettiest shade of pink and her eyebrows are delicate and her lips are lush.

Fuck. I need to talk to her, not stare at her like an imbecile.

"How much of what I just said did you hear?" I wince, bracing myself for her answer.

She laughs. "Most of it." A pause. "Fine, *all* of it."

Well, shit. "I hope I didn't hurt your feelings," I tell her.

She rests a slender hand on her chest, her lips parting dramatically. "Hurt my feelings? Never. Like I already mentioned, I do have a fondness for beastly men."

"Beastly." I keep saying the word, and it is the stupidest word alive, trust me.

She nods, her smile growing, her cheeks a faint pink. "You are rather—*large.* My father noticed you the moment we stepped into the room. Mentioned that he'd love to speak with you, if you don't mind."

"I don't mind," I immediately say. Hopefully she'll stick around and talk to me too.

I could stare at her all night.

"Perfect. I'll go and get him. Pardon me." She takes off before I can ask her name, ask who her father is, ask her anything, and I can hear Tuttle tsking behind me.

I turn and glare at him. "Thanks for practically pushing me into her."

"I don't think she minded," Tuttle drawls. "She was flirting with you."

"She was not." I refuse to get my hopes up. Can't remember the last time I flirted with a woman. And I'm talking plain, old-fashioned flirting, none of this swipe right or left app talk, or when a groupie throws herself at me and begs me to fuck her.

That's an entirely different kind of flirtation going on right there. And that's what I typically deal with.

"She totally was." Tuttle takes a sip from his drink, his gaze zeroed in just behind me. "Here they come," he warns.

I turn to find the pretty woman headed in my direction, dragging along with her an elderly gentleman who's clad in a navy-blue suit, including a vest. I see a gold chain hanging from it and I'm assuming he's carrying a...pocket watch?

I'm also assuming that's her father.

Nerves suddenly swarm me. I'm not big on meeting parents. Fathers. Mothers. Family members in general. Of course, I don't even know her, so I'm totally overreacting...

"Father, this is one of the American football players. From San Francisco?" She turns to him with a questioning look, like she's hoping he'll remember what they talked about earlier or something, and the recognition on her father's face is obvious.

"Of course, of course. It's such a pleasure to meet you." He grabs my hand and gives it a firm shake, surprising me considering he appears so old. "And your name is..."

"Cannon Whittaker," I tell him as we continue to shake hands.

"Cannon. What a name. Very—powerful. Mmmhmm." He finally releases my hand and takes a step back, his gaze sweeping over me from head to toe. "You're a giant fellow, aren't you?"

They are both watching me so closely they're making me bashful. I quickly glance over my shoulder, hoping to see sympathy on Tuttle's face, but he's nowhere to be found.

The bastard ditched me.

"I suppose so," I say as I turn to face them once more, my gaze locked on the elderly gentleman. "And you are?"

"Oh! How very rude of me," the woman says, her cheeks flushing a deep pink. "Mr. Whittaker, this is my father, the Earl of Harwood."

He's a freaking earl? I have no idea how to respond to this. And if her dad is an earl, what does that make her?

Talk about high and mighty. This girl is too much for me.

Too freaking much.

TWO

SUSANNA

THE GIANT AMERICAN football player appears at a loss for words—and social etiquette. Not that I expect him to know how to respond to the introduction of an earl. Thankfully, Father is a casual sort who can't be bothered with too much protocol.

Though he *does* enjoy a little bit of propriety, what he's due considering his position, if we're being completely honest.

"Nice to meet you," the footballer finally says, thrusting his giant hand toward my father once again. "Uh..."

"Lord Harwood," I whisper loudly, punctuated with a cheeky grin, as I'm trying to put him at ease.

Goodness, he's handsome.

"Lord Harwood," he repeats, shaking Dad's hand. For the second time.

"You're a strong sort," Dad says with a wince as he withdraws his hand. "I bet you're a terror on the field."

"Just doing my job," Mr. Whittaker says. "Sir. My lord."

I almost laugh, but I keep myself in check. His over-polite ways are cute. He's cute.

Attractive.

Even dare I think it...sexy.

Not my type at *all*.

They talk for a few minutes about football, which I find dreadfully boring. I'm not a fan of American football. The players are all so big, bulked up by the gear they wear, and it's such a violent sport.

Honestly? I'm not into sports at all. The only reason I accompanied my father to this event is because Mother's ill and didn't feel like going out this evening. She called upon me and guilted me into going, using words like, "duty," and "family."

My mother has the guilt thing down pat. She's a professional.

"Oh look! There's Alford. I need to go speak with him," Dad says, his focus on an old friend across the room, and he's gone within seconds.

Leaving me alone with the hulking American.

"He can move pretty fast when he wants," he says, amusement lacing his deep voice, his lips curled into the faintest smile.

I contemplate him, my gaze raking over him quick like, before he catches me ogling him. He's incredibly tall, I'd guess well over six foot, and he's impossibly broad. Those shoulders look like they could barrel through a brick wall and he'd come away untouched.

I'm not even going to contemplate his face again. Suffice it to say, he's handsome.

Terribly handsome.

"Yes, I suppose he can," I say, hating how nervous I sound. How nervous I feel. I'm suddenly jittery, like I just downed three cups of coffee, and my hands tend to flutter around when I get this way.

And why am I behaving like this anyway? It's not like we're alone. We're currently surrounded by at least one hundred people, possibly more, and the noise level is almost deafening.

Yet it feels like we're alone. Just the two of us facing each other, unsure of what to say next. Almost as if we're on a...

Date.

"You never did tell me your name," he says, breaking the ice.

"Oh, sorry." I smile and hold out my hand. "Lady Susanna Sumner."

"Lady Susanna Sumner," he repeats slowly. I like the way he says my name, how it sounds. He takes my hand and gives it the briefest shake, followed by a too-long squeeze. "It's very nice to meet you."

I slowly withdraw my hand from his, feeling as if I'm in a trance. My fingers and palm tingle from where they made contact with his, and the heat in his blue eyes is unmistakable, even for an unseasoned, mostly relationship-less woman like me.

He's interested.

In *me*.

What a strange—and pleasant—turn of events.

"It's a pleasure to meet you too," I say, my voice weak.

It's his turn to smile, and oh, what a dazzler it is. It transforms his entire face, lighting it up, making him look young and sweet, and I wonder if that's just a ruse. Someone as large as he is who's a professional athlete can't be considered *sweet*. Can he? "What do people call you?"

I blink at him. "Pardon me?"

"What do your—*friends* call you? Or your acquaintances? What with the title and all." Cannon—such an unusual name—waves a hand toward me.

He sounds genuinely curious. In England, amongst the social circles I move in, Lady This-and-That isn't rare. We are a dime a dozen. My title doesn't mean a thing to those who know me, or know of me.

But an American who probably has no idea how nobility works? He might be impressed.

Cannon Whittaker? He definitely looks impressed.

"Formally, I'm referred to as *my lady*, or even Lady Susanna," I tell him.

"No shit?" His cheeks turn ruddy and I'm tempted to laugh again. "Uh, sorry about that."

I wave a jittery hand. "No need to apologize."

"I shouldn't curse in front of you."

"Not like I haven't heard it before." My older brother's colorful language comes to mind.

"Do they call you Lady Sumner?" he asks.

It takes me a second to process his quick change of subject. "No, I'm afraid not." I shake my head.

"Why?" He tilts his head to the side, like a curious puppy.

"That's..." I don't really have a good reason as to why. "Not how it's done."

"According to who?" He sounds surprised.

"The peerage."

"What's the peerage?" Now he sounds really confused.

I smile, putting on a bright face. He does not want me to get into a conversation about the peerage. Talk about dull. "It really doesn't matter. Just a bunch of boring rules."

He steps closer, his gaze intense, his voice shifting lower. "What do you want *me* to call you?"

His nearness sends the jitters flying away, replacing them with a slow, yearning tremble. "I suppose you can call me... Susanna?" I offer, my voice weak.

His smile is slow. Intimate. Seeing it sets my skin on fire. "Then that's what I'll call you." He pauses for effect, I'm sure. "Susanna."

Oh.

Dear.

I'm in trouble.

I want to fan myself, but I keep my hands firmly at my sides. Plastering on a smile, I meet his gaze once more. "Are you ready for your game tomorrow?"

He shrugs those massive shoulders. "As ready as I'll ever be."

We go silent for a moment and my brain scrambles to keep up the conversation.

"Have you been to London before?" I ask.

"Never." He shakes his head. "I don't get to travel outside of the country much."

"Oh. Me either, I'm afraid," I say ruefully. It's my biggest regret. I would love to travel the world. I've done the European jaunt in ten days, where you go to the highlight cities and see the tourist sites, but I've always yearned to see more of the world.

Maybe someday.

"You don't? That's surprising."

"Why do you say that?" I ask, genuinely curious.

"I figured someone of your...social stature would travel a lot," he answers.

"Just because my father is an earl doesn't mean that we have loads of money." The moment the words fall from my lips, I want to shove them back in. I am a Sumner. We don't talk about our finances. It's no one's business but our own.

Though we do have money. We just don't like to speak of it.

"Really? Can't you, like, sell a crown or something?"

He appears downright baffled.

And I can't help it, I start to laugh.

Uncontrollably.

After a few seconds of helpless silence, he joins in, hesitantly at first, and then we're both on a roll. I'm laughing so much, I'm clutching my stomach, and I have tears in my eyes. Oh, and people are starting to stare. Normally, I would straighten up by now, aware that I was on display and making a fool of myself, but I don't straighten up. Not at all.

It's as if I can't stop.

Cannon is no help. His booming laugh encourages mine, and as people walk past us, they smile helplessly. Some of them even laugh along with us, like they're in on the joke.

But they're not.

It's just us. Cannon and I. Sharing a private joke that probably wasn't even that funny, yet I don't care.

I like it.

I like *him*.

THREE

CANNON

LADY SUSANNA'S laugh is beautiful. Infectious. Normally I'd be insulted by someone laughing at me for what I said. I'm not the smartest guy in the room, not by a long shot, but I always tried hard in school. I still try hard in life. Shit doesn't come easy for me, it never has. And when it comes to my smarts—or lack thereof—I'm a little sensitive sometimes.

But I know in my gut she's not laughing at me like I'm an idiot. My selling a crown comment made her laugh because, let's face it. That shit is kind of funny. I mean, seriously, what the hell am I even talking about?

I have no idea what to do with this girl. And besides, why is she talking to me? She's in a totally different realm, and that realm is way above mine.

"Does your family actually have crowns?" I ask after the laughter has finally died and we've somewhat composed ourselves.

She dabs at her eyes, a little hiccup escaping her. "Actually, we do. Sort of. They're called tiaras, really, and only the women wear them. But we can't sell them."

"Why the hell not? I bet they're worth a lot."

"Oh I'm sure. But they're part of the family jewels." She waves a dismissive hand, like that one sentence should explain everything.

I chuckle, my stomach aching too much to burst into full-blown laughter again. "Family jewels? Don't those, uh, belong to your father? Maybe your brother, if you have one?"

Her cheeks go red and she covers her giggling mouth. "You're funny."

I puff out my chest at her compliment. "Thanks."

"But rude," she adds, dropping her hand as she composes herself once more.

She's not wrong there.

I glance around the crowded room, wishing we were anywhere but here. We should go. I want to talk to her some more.

Alone.

Grabbing hold of her arm, I tug her in close, so I can whisper in her ear. "Want to get out of here?"

A shiver moves through her and she pulls away slightly, those luminous blue eyes gazing up at me, her expression serious. "Where would we go?"

"I don't know." I shrug. "Find a bar and have some drinks? Or maybe grab some dinner?" Lord knows we could find better food than what they're serving here, and I'm fucking starving. "There's gotta be a couple of decent restaurants nearby, right?"

"Quite a few of them actually," she says with a nod.

"Then we'll go to whatever restaurant you recommend." I smile at her. "Somewhere nice and quiet."

She frowns. "But what about my father?"

Please tell me she doesn't want to bring her dad to dinner with us. "Did you drive him here or somethin'?" I ask, fighting the frustration running through me. I just want to leave. With her. And I don't want any obstacle blocking me either.

"No, he actually drove me," she answers, glancing around, like she's looking for him.

Shit. The hairs on the back of my neck prickle as I realize something. I don't even know how old she is. What if she's…

"How old are you exactly?" I ask, my voice gruff. I take a deep breath, fighting the panic rising within me.

If she says eighteen, I'm out.

"Twenty-three." She's still frowning. So hard, there are little lines in her forehead, and she pulls out of my hold. "Wait, did you think I was underage?"

"Maybe." I shrug again. She's younger than me, but at least she's legal, thank God. "Most twenty-three-year-old women I know don't need to ask their father's permission to go anywhere."

She stands a little straighter, her eyes narrowing, her lips forming into a thin line. I don't think she liked that I said that.

Worse, I kind of feel like shit for saying it, too.

"I don't need to ask his *permission*," she says, her tone haughty. "I just—we came together. And I certainly don't want to abandon him. Telling him I'm leaving with someone else is the polite thing to do."

"Sure. I get it." I scrub a hand along my jaw, trying to come up with the right thing to say. "Maybe you could send him a text."

Susanna scoffs. "He never checks his text messages. I'm not even sure if he brought his phone with him."

Impossible. Everyone I know is constantly on their phone. "Well, let's go find him then."

"How about *I* go find him?" She's smiling at me once again, and seeing it makes me feel like I've won the big one—not Super Bowl intensity, but close. Playoff intensity for sure. She keeps looking at me like that, and I'll probably let her do whatever she wants. "Give me a few minutes. I'll search him out and let him know I'm leaving with you."

Shock hits me right between the eyes and I blink at her. "You really want to go to dinner? With me?"

Jesus, I sound like a complete idiot. But she makes me feel like one, so it's like I can't help myself.

"Yes." Her eyes are bright. I swear they're twinkling, like she's amused. "I do. Want to go to dinner with you."

With that, she turns on her heel and disappears into the swelling crowd. I watch her blonde head move through the clusters of people until she gradually disappears, and the moment I lose sight of her, I'm off to find a bathroom, where I can take a quick piss and assess the situation.

Minutes later I'm at the sink washing my hands, staring at my reflection, wondering what she might see in me. I'm all right looking. Not movie star handsome like Jordan Tuttle, and I'm not classically handsome like my teammate Tucker McCloud either. Those are the two most popular players on our team—the ones who the ladies scream and cry and generally freak the fuck out over.

Me? The one thing I've got going for me is my body. I'm tall. Broad. Muscular. Probably intimidating, though I don't mean to be.

Well, that's a damn lie. I try my best to intimidate every motherfucker I face out on the football field.

Sometimes I'm a little awkward, like I don't know my own strength, which is true. I have to be careful so I don't scare the ladies. And while I realize I'm not the guy to make all the girls' panties wet, I do know I'm okay looking.

I guess.

Turning my head this way and that, I check out my profile. I shaved carefully tonight, so there aren't any stray hairs. I have a few scars I don't even notice anymore, I've had them so long, but did Susanna notice?

Did they turn her off?

She's leaving with you, dumbass, so she must see something in your ugly mug.

I stare into the mirror straight on, my gaze dropping to my crooked nose. Broke that more than once, and I'm probably going to need surgery on it eventually. My hair has grown darker over the years, most of the dark blond from my youth gone, though my mother constantly tells me I should dye it.

Hell no. I'm not that much of a vain motherfucker.

Overall, I'm a pretty simple guy. I like food, action movies and pretty women. Oh, and I love football. Some might look at me and see nothing but a hulking mass of flesh, and that's okay. I'm not offended. And hey, there's plenty of other guys in the NFL—hell, in any professional sport—who look just like my ass.

So what's this fancy British girl see in me?

I dry my hands and haul ass out of the bathroom, thankful it wasn't far from where Lady Susanna Sumner—damn, that's a mouthful—last saw me. The room is even more crowded now, and the dull roar of conversation and clinking of glasses is starting to make my head hurt.

I want out of here. Stat.

More than anything, I want to find a small, cozy restaurant with tiny tables—or even better, tiny booths—so me and Susanna have to sit nice and close to each other and there's a candle on the table and the light flickers across her beautiful face and...

Yep, I'm getting way ahead of myself. Caught up in my own fantasy. First things first, I gotta find the star of my intimate dinner fantasy before I can hightail it out of here.

But I don't see her pretty little blonde head anywhere.

Defeat smacks me in the chest, and my shoulders sag. Did she ditch me? I sort of acted like an asshole earlier, about her coming with her dad. Can't blame her if she's pissed at me, which means I guess I can't blame her if she left the party either. I should ask Tuttle to give me lessons in class.

More like lessons on when to keep my mouth shut.

"There you are."

I turn at the sound of her voice, smiling in relief when I see her. "Sorry, ducked into the bathroom real quick," I tell her.

The light dims in her eyes a little bit and I wonder if that was a mistake, mentioning the bathroom. But damn it, we're all God's creatures, and we all gotta go. What's the big deal?

"Are you ready to leave?" she asks.

"Definitely." I offer my arm to her, but she doesn't take it.

"Isn't there someone you should tell?" I frown at her words. "Someone you need to inform that you're leaving?"

"They don't care."

"But this party is for you," she says slowly.

"It's for all of us. The entire team," I return just as slowly. "I'm one of many, and they won't miss me. I'm not even the most popular one."

She looks shocked. "Really? You're not one of the most popular on your team?"

"Really," I say with a firm nod, taking her arm since she won't take mine. "Let's get out of here. I'll text someone later. Let them know where I went."

I escort her out of the building before she can say another word.

FOUR

SUSANNA

I SCROLL through my phone and find the address to a restaurant I know is not too far from the party and then enter it in my Uber app. The car appears before us in less than two minutes, and he drops us off at the restaurant in another five. Somehow in those last five minutes, the air becomes bitterly cold, and when Cannon opens the car door for me, a shiver takes over my body just before I exit.

Cannon, of course, notices.

"Cold?" he asks as I stop to stand beside him, his voice a low, deep murmur that warms my insides. I'm not wearing a coat—a rather stupid decision, but going out this evening had been such a last-minute thing, I completely forgot.

"A little bit," I tell him, sounding as if I'm in a daze.

I blame the daze thing on having him so close, especially in the confines of the small car. His body radiates heat like a furnace, so maybe that's why the night air felt so chilly.

"Come here," he tells me as we head for the front door of the restaurant. He lifts his arm, swoops me under it and tugs me close to his side. "I'll warm you up."

I say nothing as we make those too-few steps to the door, savoring the sensation of having him plastered next to me. He smells amazing—like good, clean man. Plus, he's solid as a rock. All muscle. So tall I barely reach his shoulder—I barely reach his chest—and I'm not what I would call a short person.

But Cannon Whittaker? He makes me feel tiny.

He drops his arm from my shoulders as he reaches for the door to open it, and I ignore the disappointment crashing through me as I walk through the door first. The disappointment disappears in an instant, though, when I feel his large hand gently press against my lower back. He guides me toward the front desk, both of us smiling at the hostess watching our arrival. Within seconds, she's ushering us deep into the restaurant, to a small table that's near the back of the room. We sit and she hands the menus to us, listing the specials for the evening before she dashes away to take care of another customer.

I can't recall a single thing she said.

"I'm starving," Cannon says as he wrenches open the menu, his gaze eagerly scanning the restaurant's offerings. The menus are tall, encased in black leather, and Cannon's hands span practically the entire thing.

I stare at them, his long fingers, his wide palms, completely entranced. Are his hands smooth or rough? I'd bet rough, since he handles footballs all day long.

Does he literally handle them all day long? My thoughts are an exaggeration, I'm sure. Doesn't deter me from thinking his hands are manly, though. I bet if they'd smooth over my dress, they might snag on the fabric. Does he have callouses?

A little shiver moves through me. None of the men I've dated have rough hands. They definitely don't have callouses. The men I've dated either work in offices or lounge around spending their family's money.

"Have you been here before?" he asks a few seconds later, knocking me from my lusty thoughts of his hands.

On my body.

"Oh." I startle, shaking my head. Swallow the sudden lump in my throat. "Yes, I have," I say as I nonchalantly open the menu, my gaze going blurry when I try to read my options. I'm not particularly hungry. More like I'm too distracted by the handsome man sitting across from me. "Once."

"Was it any good?" His gaze never strays from the menu, which makes me want to laugh. He's not even paying attention to me, yet he's all I can think about.

"Delicious," I say with heavy emphasis, finally causing him to finally glance up. His blue gaze meets mine, warm and friendly, and he winks before he returns his attention to the stupid menu.

I've always thought winking was silly. But I like the way he winked at me just now.

I like it a lot.

"I came here on a date," I continue, trying to draw his attention back to me. "My ex-boyfriend brought me here."

Well. A *tiny* fib. He wasn't my ex-boyfriend. More like a man I went on a couple of dates with. One day, we just stopped texting each other. And that was that.

"An ex?" Cannon asks the menu. "How long did you two go out?"

I'm tempted to say years, but that might be a bit much. "Months," I tell him, which isn't exactly a lie. Our three dates—or was it actually four?—spread out over about six weeks' time total.

"Are you telling me the restaurant holds a lot of memories for you?"

He is still looking at his menu, when I wish he was looking at me instead. What's so fascinating about his meal options?

"Yes," I tell him, snapping my menu shut and slapping it onto the table. "I'm remembering all the good times with Richard as we speak."

This, *this* finally gets Cannon's attention. His gaze meets mine, his expression...amused? "Richard? That's your ex's name?"

I nod, trying my best to keep my expression neutral. "He's the heir to an earldom, like my father."

"Lucky Dick," Cannon says just before he starts chuckling.

"That's what his family called him," I say, refusing to laugh with him.

But it is a little funny.

"What? They called him a lucky dick? Are you serious?" Cannon's laughter grows.

"No, no. They called him Dickie. That's his nickname," I explain, my lips curling into a smile despite my faint annoyance.

Why am I annoyed again? Because the poor man is hungry and is trying to figure out what he wants to eat?

I'm being absolutely ridiculous.

"*Dickie?* Oh shit, that's even worse." His laughter dies, his expression somber as he considers me. "You actually went out with a guy you called Dickie? To his face?"

"I didn't call him Dickie, his family did. I called him Richard." I take a sip of my water, wondering at our round-about conversations. We tend to veer off track easily. Is it because we're from two different countries? Do we not have common interests? Opposites attract and all that, but are we *too* opposite?

"Richard, Dick, Dickie, it's all the same to me." Cannon closes his menu and sets it on the table in front of him. "Let me guess. He was a total jerk."

"Not really," I say with a little shrug. "More like he was…"

"Arrogant."

"No."

"A womanizer."

I make a face. I can't imagine Richard dating loads of women at the same time. He wasn't that charming. "Not at all."

"A real smug bastard," Cannon suggests eagerly, like he wants Richard to be a terrible, awful human being.

"Not even close. He was just." I offer another shrug as my mind scrambles for the most accurate thing to say. "Very...boring."

"Oh." Cannon actually looks disappointed. "I thought with a name like that, and him being an earldom or whatever, he'd be a snobby prick."

I don't bother correcting Cannon in his use of earldom. I don't even flinch at his use of the words *snobby prick*. Instead, I think back on those past three dates with Richard.

His wispy light brown hair that was fast receding even though he wasn't quite thirty. His brown eyes and thin, hard mouth. The way he always spoke of his mother, as if she ran his life—which I suppose she did. He worked in finance and it was apparent from the start how much he hated his job. Was merely waiting for his father to pass so he could take over the title. He had plans on opening the family estate to the public so they could earn money, and his mother was aghast at the mere suggestion.

He wasn't looking for the love of his life or the woman of his dreams. He was merely looking for a countess to take care of the future estate.

"He was snobbish," I concede. "But I wouldn't call him a..."

"Prick?" Cannon finishes for me.

"Right." I'm not used to saying such things in front of a man. Especially a man I'm trying to impress. Flirt with.

Of course, this is a man who I will most likely never see again after tonight, so I can be whoever I want to be if I really want to.

The idea flits through my head, flashing bright like one of those giant signs in Piccadilly Circus.

You can be whoever you want to be.

Our server magically appears, an older gentleman with graying temples and a wide smile. "Good evening. May I start you out with something to drink?"

"Do you have champagne?" I ask.

"We do. Would you care for a glass or a bottle?"

"We can get a bottle," Cannon says firmly, his gaze meeting mine for the briefest moment before he looks up at the server. "And I'll take a beer."

My mind shifts as the server lists the various beers they serve, excitement coursing through me at the promise this evening suddenly holds. The idea of doing whatever I want, being whomever I want sounds...exhilarating.

Thrilling, even.

I'm so used to portraying a certain role. Lady Susanna Sumner. Youngest child of the Earl of Harwood. Dull, dutiful daughter who jumps whenever her parents ask her to do something. I did well in school, I traveled throughout Europe before I turned twenty and now I work a nice little job at an art gallery in London, all while waiting for a proper man to come along and sweep me off my feet like I'm Cinderella or something.

Waiting for my prince.

Or a marquess or duke or whatever.

Just thinking about what I've done these last few years makes me want to yawn.

I go still, the only thing moving my eyelids as I blink again and again.

Oh my. My life has become so...*boring*.

The realization is startling.

My attention returns to Cannon, who is currently studying the back of the menu. Hmm. He's quite attractive in a large, American way. As I've already thought, not my normal type, but I'm open to change.

I'm open to anything at this moment.

Tonight, I'm sitting across from a sexy American. An American celebrity, a *football player* who could probably crush me with his hands if he wanted to.

But he doesn't want to. He's watching me right now, an unfamiliar gleam in his eye as he contemplates me.

"What are you thinking?" I ask, surprising myself. I would normally never ask a man a question like that. But tonight is for new adventures.

When my champagne arrives, I'll definitely drink to that.

FIVE

CANNON

"I'M THINKING about how beautiful you are," I answer Susanna truthfully. She really is stunning, in that classic, elegant way some women can be. She's just very...refined? Is that the right word? Her cheekbones and jaw are sharp, her nose is straight, her blue eyes are extra bright and her full lips are the color of a classic red rose.

And now her cheeks are the color of pink roses, thanks to the compliment I just gave her.

"Thank you. That's very sweet of you to say," she murmurs, casting her gaze downward for a brief moment before she lifts her head. "I can't believe we're here. Together."

"Why do you say that?" I feel the same way, but want to hear her reasoning first before I make any confessions.

"You're not my type," she blurts, covering her mouth after the words escape, her eyes wide. Slowly, she drops her hand, her expression sheepish. "Not that there's anything wrong with you."

I raise an eyebrow. "Gee, thanks."

Her cheeks turn redder. "Oh goodness, I'm not trying to insult you, I just—I'm making a mess of this, and I apologize. What I meant to say is..." She takes a deep breath, exhaling loudly before she continues. "You're not the type of man I normally date, but there's something good to be said in that."

She's not the type I normally go for either, that's for damn sure. She's too prim, too proper, too sweet. "Like what?"

"There's nothing wrong with trying something a little different sometimes. Clearly who I've been dating in the past hasn't worked, since I'm still single," she says with a self-depreciating laugh.

"Like Dickie, your ex-boyfriend?" I ask with a wince.

That is the damn worst name on the planet, I swear.

"Oh, it was never too serious with Dickie, and yes that definitely didn't work." She waves a hand. Laughs again. "That was a long time ago, though."

"How long?"

"I don't know. Six months? Nine?" She tilts her head, as if she's quietly counting back the months. "Eight months, actually. During the winter. He told me I was a bright light on a cold, dreary day once. That was nice."

For some godforsaken reason, jealousy rises within me, making me clench my fists in my lap. "I guess he's a goddamned poet."

I would never think to say something like that to a woman. I'm not one to say a bunch of flowery nonsense to get between a woman's legs. I'm a little more direct.

She seems startled by my response. "Oh, he wasn't a poet. Not at all. That was probably the nicest thing he ever said to me while we dated."

Huh. Well, I guess that makes me feel a little better, but not much.

And why the hell do I care what her ex-boyfriend said to her? This is a one-shot deal. I'll take her to dinner, hopefully kiss her a little bit in the back of an Uber, maybe even feel her up a little bit too, and then we're done. I'll play my game tomorrow, we'll win because that's what we do, and then head back home.

End of story.

The server returns to the table with our drinks, making an elaborate show of popping the cork on the bottle of Veuve Clicquot before pouring us each a glass. I didn't want any champagne, but when Susanna lifts her glass toward me in a toast, I grab mine and clink our glasses together.

"To new friends," she says, smiling prettily.

"New friends," I agree, downing most of the champagne in one swallow, making a face when I'm done. The alcohol fizzes in my throat, and I know I'm going to burp something good in a few minutes. Beer does that to me too.

Of course, I absolutely should not burp at all in front of Lady Susanna. I need to watch myself.

We order our meals—steak for me, trout for her—and make idle chitchat while we nibble on our appetizer, some sort of meat and cheese tray Susanna highly recommended, as did the waiter.

I'm just along for the ride on this dinner date tonight. The menu was in English and I still had a hard time reading it. The way they described the entrees was sort of confusing. I drink both the champagne and the beer, and the server brings me another one when I request it. Before our meals even arrive, I'm feeling nice and toasty.

Okay, maybe I'm buzzing, but so is Susanna. I can tell by her flushed cheeks and the way her eyes sparkle extra bright. Her voice is getting louder too, and when I tell her a joke right after the server delivers our entrees, she bursts into laughter so loud, people turn to stare at us.

"Uh oh. I'm getting a little out of control," she singsongs, giggling as she grabs her fork and knife and starts carving into her trout. Which has the head still on it, I might add.

I glance down at my steak, eternally thankful no sad cow face is staring up at me. "I kind of like it when you get a little out of control," I tell her, cutting off a slice of steak and popping it into my mouth.

Damn. The meat is so tender, it practically melts in my mouth.

She goes completely still. "Really? You actually like me this way?"

I nod and keep eating, my stomach demanding more.

"Even though I'm being loud and obnoxious?" When I don't say anything, she continues, "Those are my parents' least favorite traits in a person. When they're loud and obnoxious."

"Oh come on. Everyone gets a little loud and obnoxious sometimes," I say after I swallow. Some more than others. I've been known to behave that way a time or two.

Or twenty.

"No." She's shaking her head. "Not my parents. They are the epitome of well-behaved nobility. They are completely unruffled at all times. Nothing bothers them. They don't drink too much, eat too much, or talk too much. In fact, those are their rules."

"Their rules?" Every parent has rules, I get that. I was raised by a single mama, and she just wanted the best for me.

Just do your best, was always something she said. *And stay out of trouble.*

That's it. And guess what? I did my damn best, and I tried as much as possible to stay out of trouble—except for those years in high school when I was causing as much trouble as possible and never getting caught.

But I learned from that. Trouble gets you nowhere. Doing right is what sets you on the upward path.

Susanna nods enthusiastically. "When I was younger, I wanted to be *just* like them."

"And you don't want to be like them now?"

"I don't think I *could* be like them now," she admits, her teeth sinking into her lower lip. I stare at that lip, momentarily entranced. The little move is sexy, I can't deny it. "I'd most likely fail. I'm afraid I'm not quite up to their exacting standards."

I set my silverware on the edge of the white plate, my appetite satisfied for the moment. "You want me to be honest with you?"

She nods once more, her eyes wide as she stares at me, her lips forming into a delectable pout. The candlelight flickers across her face, casting her in faint shadows, and I'm suddenly seized with the need to grab hold of her and kiss her senseless. "Absolutely," she breathes.

"Here's a little secret." I lean across the table and she mimics my movement, meeting me halfway, our gazes never straying. "Your parents aren't perfect."

Susanna blinks at me, but doesn't say a word.

"No one is perfect," I continue. "Not your parents, not me, not you. We all have flaws. And the only one who believes you can't do something is...you."

I brace myself for her to say I insulted her the longer she remains silent. A lot of people don't want to hear this kind of stuff. They think I'm being rude, too harsh, whatever.

I'm just being real.

Eventually, her lips curve. "Who are you? Some sort of self-help guru?"

I shrug, all of a sudden embarrassed. "Not even. I just know when to—believe in myself."

"Is that how you became a professional football player?" she asks. "By believing in yourself?"

"That and working damn hard every single day. I lived and breathed football all through high school and college," I say, grabbing my silverware and starting in on my steak again.

"What you're telling me is that you're the type of man to go after what you want," she continues.

"Yeah. Because if I don't, someone else will," I say, taking another bite of my steak.

"Hmm." She taps her index finger against her lips before she grabs her wineglass. "I like that," she says before she takes a drink.

Pride flashes through me. Something about having her approval is a total turn on.

Crazy, right? Like, why should I care what this woman thinks? She's hot and I'm attracted to her, but I know, this won't go anywhere, and that's facts. I'm leaving this city in a few days, and I'll never see her again, unless it's over social media or text.

Susanna lives in another country, for the love of God.

I can't pursue this.

We spend the remainder of our dinner discussing my football career. She seems truly fascinated, asking lots of questions, curious about what position I play and everything I did to get where I am today. I tell her everything I can think of, probably too much, but it's not every day I have a woman interested in football. Interested in everything I've done over the years.

Flat out interested in *me*.

I mean, yeah, there are women who *claim* they're interested and like to talk about the big football player, but it always feels like they're faking it. It's as if they think they have to pretend they're into me, or otherwise it feels like they're just using me for my body or my fame.

Pretty sure most of the time that's exactly what they're doing.

She gets me talking about myself so much, I realize as we're leaving the restaurant that I never really asked much about her, which makes me feel like a shit, and I tell her so as we climb in the back of the Uber Black car I ordered.

"You must think I'm a total ass," I say with a shake of my head as the car pulls away from the curb.

"What do you mean? Why would I think that?" She touches my forearm, seemingly concerned.

I feel her touch as if she branded me. My entire body flashes hot.

All because she touched me on my freaking *arm*.

"I went on and on about myself and never once asked a question about you. Talk about a jerk thing to do," I mutter, my voice extra gruff. Maybe it's the beer I've been drinking, but I feel extremely bad. Like over-the-top bad, which is probably silly.

Maybe it's the jet lag catching up with me.

"There's no need for you to apologize. Really." She smiles up at me and I stare at her, hypnotized. Christ, she's pretty. In that untouchable-yet-I-just-want-to-mess-her-up kind of way. "I enjoyed learning so much about you."

The sincerity in her voice rings true. She means it.

"Maybe, uh, we could talk some more." I hesitate, wondering if I'm asking too much. "There's a nice bar back at my hotel."

Her delicate brows lift the slightest bit, indicating my question has surprised her. But I had to ask.

I had to.

"It's okay," I say when she still hasn't answered me. "Maybe another time."

There will be no other time. I will play my game, I will leave this country, and I will never see her again. This is a one-shot thing. I know it.

She knows it.

"No." She squeezes my forearm, and I resist the urge to haul her into my arms. "I mean, yes. I'd love to go back to your hotel with you."

"Your father won't mind?" Aw jeez, I'm asking about her dad like we're in high school or something.

She laughs and shakes her head. "No, of course he won't mind. It's not like I live with my parents. I have my own flat."

Oh. Well.

That changes everything.

SIX

SUSANNA

I CAN'T STOP SQUEEZING Cannon's arm, silently marveling at how warm he is, how incredibly solid he feels beneath my palm. I remember when he swooped me under his arm before we entered the restaurant, how hot and firm his body felt pressed next to mine.

A shiver moves through me at the memory.

The car is silent, save for the quietly playing radio and the windshield wipers squeaking against the glass. The Uber driver doesn't say a word, too busy concentrating on the busy street and the rain, and I'm suddenly filled with the need to...oh, I don't know. Throw myself at this giant man and see if he'll catch me?

He'd catch me. I can pretty much guarantee it.

"Think it'll rain tomorrow during the game?" he asks, his deep voice interrupting the quiet.

"Doubtful." Nervous laughter escapes me and I clamp my lips shut when I realize how silly I sound. "It seems to rain almost every evening lately, and since your game is in the afternoon, you should be fine, just a little cloudy. Besides, most of the time the rain is really just mist from low-hanging clouds. It's always so dreary here, especially this time of year."

"Kind of like San Francisco," he muses.

"I hear it can get quite foggy there." I release my hold on him and settle more comfortably in my seat, hyper aware of Cannon sitting next to me. So close, yet not quite touching. His body heat radiates, tempting me to snuggle closer, but I keep myself firmly planted.

"Mmm hmm. You have your own place, huh?" he asks.

He seemed startled by my earlier revelation, which in turn surprised me. I guess he thought I still lived at home? I moved out at the ripe age of nineteen, unable to take it anymore at my parents' grand country estate. It's a beautiful place, don't get me wrong, and I have such fond memories of my childhood, but when you're in your late teens yearning to break free and make it in the big city, well, you...

Get the hell away from that grand country estate and move yourself into a tiny, leaky flat in London.

"It's nothing special," I tell him with a wave of my hand. "It's very small. And you have to climb four flights of stairs to get to my front door."

"Not a problem. I'm a guy who loves a challenge." He grins, his teeth extra white in the dim light of the car. "I can handle a couple of flights of stairs."

"Hoping to see my flat, hmm?" I'm teasing him, but...is he really hoping to see where I live?

Excitement makes my blood heat, and I mentally tell myself to calm down. There won't be a chance for him to see my flat. He's leaving soon. Perhaps we'll indulge in some...

Kissing?

Touching?

Fondling?

My blood runs hotter at the thought of his hands on my body. Am I being too hopeful?

"Sure," he says easily, and that ease, plus the hopeful look on his handsome face, almost feels false.

Or maybe that's my own self-doubt creeping in.

We arrive at Cannon's hotel in a matter of minutes, and next thing I know he's leaping out of the car, rounding the back of it to hold my door open. He takes my hand and helps me out, pulling me close and leading me into the hotel with my hand still clasped in his. The very hand that is so large, mine practically disappears.

The man is massive. I can't imagine what he might look like without a stitch of clothing on.

A shiver moves through me at the mental image. Then again, I might like to imagine Cannon naked. I'm sure he's incredibly muscular, not an ounce of fat on him, while I'm a little more on the large-breasted and curvy-bottomed side of things. I can look sleek and refined when I need to, but that's only because I'm strapped into the most confining bra known to woman.

Wait a minute. My brain takes off in that direction. Yes, we just might—mess around, and my undergarments aren't very sexy.

Like at all.

Oh dear.

"Why are you frowning? Having second thoughts?"

Cannon's concerned voice pulls me from my brain, and I shake my head, smiling up at him as we head toward the bar on the other side of the hotel's expansive lobby. "No. Of course not."

He studies me for a moment, his gaze razor sharp. "Why do I get the feeling you're lying to me?"

"I would never lie to you," I tell him sincerely, which is the truth. I'm not a liar. I never have been. Some people tell me I'm honest almost to a fault.

"Then you're—fibbing. You're trying to cover up something, I can tell." He comes to a halt in front of the mostly empty, open front bar, causing me to stop walking as well. "I know what's wrong."

"You do?" My voice is hollow, and I clear my throat, reminding myself to look and seem positive. Confident.

"You're nervous."

I sigh, my shoulders slumping. All pretense of confidence floats away. "Is it that obvious?"

"Yeah, but don't take that as an insult. I'm guessing you don't usually do this sort of thing." When I don't speak, he continues, "Like hang out in hotel bars with random foreign dudes."

"Foreign dudes?" I start to laugh. "No, I don't usually do this sort of thing."

More like I've *never* done this sort of thing. Not with a man I've met at a club, or on a blind date, and especially never while I was in school.

He takes a step closer, so close his chest is almost pressed to mine. I have to tilt my head back to meet his gaze. "If you don't want to do this, I can arrange for a car to take you home." When I say nothing, he carries on. "I don't want to make you uncomfortable."

My heart melts. He is the sweetest. "Let's go have a drink," I say as I reach for both of his hands and hold them in mine.

His gaze never wavers. "Are you sure?"

My brows shoot up. "Are you trying to convince me to leave?"

His answer is swift, his smile...adorable. "Hell no."

"Buy me a drink then." I return his smile, and without warning, he leans down, brushing his mouth against mine so quickly, I could almost imagine the kiss didn't happen.

But it did. And the touch of his soft, warm lips on mine sends a shockwave throughout my whole body.

All the way to my toes.

We stay in the hotel bar for over an hour, until we're the only people left and the bartender is sending us not-so-subtle *get out of here* looks as he repeatedly wipes down the counters, his arm working in furious circles.

"We should go," I tell Cannon, my voice reluctant, my gaze lingering on his expressive face. It's been such a joy talking with him. Smiling when he smiles, laughing when he laughs, touching him when he touches me.

His touches aren't too forward, and neither are his words, and for once in my life, I want a man to be more forward. I get the sense, though, that he's reining himself in, for fear I might scare easily? I'm not sure.

I've given him all the signs. I'm flirty. I touch his arm a lot. Once I had another drink in me, I dared to touch his knee. Three times. His thigh, twice.

And let me just say his thigh was rock hard and so incredibly warm. My cheeks are heating just thinking about it.

"You're blushing," Cannon says, humor lacing his voice. I meet his gaze, a nervous laugh escaping me before I look away. "And you have to tell me why."

"It's too embarrassing." I wave a hand, my fingers almost brushing his nose, we're sitting so close. The low armchairs in the back of the bar allow for very intimate conversation. I'm sure it was purposely planned.

"Now you definitely have to tell me why." He reaches out, tucking a wayward strand of hair behind my ear, his fingers brushing against my skin and making me shiver. "Come on. Don't hold out on me."

I decide to draw this out. "Do you really want to know?"

"Hell yeah I do," he says without hesitation.

Tipping my head closer to him, I lean in, my gaze zeroed in on his. "I was remembering what your—thigh felt like earlier, when I touched you."

"Really." His voice is gruff, and his eyes flare with heat.

I nod. "Really."

"Want to know what I was thinking when you touched my thigh?" His voice has somehow gone even lower, a delicious rumbling along my nerve endings that makes me shiver in anticipation, and I nod slowly, like I'm in a trance.

"How much I wanted your hand to slide up a little higher."

My gaze drops to his crotch as if I have no control over myself, and he chuckles, though there is no humor in the sound.

"You keep looking at me like that and I swear I'll pop a tent right here in the bar," he threatens.

I briefly press my lips together as I return my gaze to his. "The only one who'll see it is me."

"And the bartender."

"He's not paying attention to us." God, I hope not.

"He's glaring at us yet again right now."

I chance a glance over my shoulder to discover Cannon is right. The bartender is glowering in our direction.

"We should go," I repeat once I face Cannon again.

He lifts his brows. "Ready for me to get you a car?"

"No." I shake my head, a nervous smile trembling on my lips. "I sort of hoped we could—go back to your room."

His brows rise even higher. "You sure about that?"

I nod silently. My sudden nerves make me afraid I might say something stupid so I remain quiet.

"Let's go." He grabs my hand and hauls me out of the chair, practically dragging me across the expansive hotel lobby, he's walking so fast. We stop at the bank of lifts, Cannon stabbing the up button with his index finger, his other hand still curled around mine.

Impatience radiates off his large body and I glance up at him to find him already watching me, his eyes swirling with unknown emotion as he studies me. His expression is downright thunderous, his lips thin in pure determination.

My own lips part, and I'm about to say something when the doors slide open. We enter the empty car, Cannon reaching out to press the six button repeatedly. The doors close, the elevator starts its ascent, and the next thing I know, I'm being pressed against the wall, Cannon's arms wrapped around my waist, his body pinning mine.

He covers me so completely I feel and see nothing but him. Glancing up, I catch him in mid-descent, his mouth hovering above mine for the longest second of my life before our lips finally touch. And the moment that happens, it's like we've ignited a spark. Flipped a switch and turned up the flame.

This is no tentative, hesitant kiss from a new suitor—the types of actual first kisses I'm used to. No, Cannon's kiss is hungry. Insistent. His mouth is firm yet soft, his lips parted, his tongue eagerly searching for and finding mine. I let him devour me, and the longer it goes on, the more I try my best to devour him in return. I slide my hands up his hard chest, my fingers clutching at the fabric of the shirt, and somewhere in the distance I hear a soft ding, but I refuse to let him go.

"We're at my floor," he murmurs against my lips, and I hear a disappointed whimper at his words.

I realize quickly the whimper came from me.

He slips his arm around my shoulders and guides me out of the lift, turning right and leading me down the hall. My head is spinning as we walk, my lips tingling, my entire body feels like it's caught on fire. I don't even know how I manage to walk to his room, but suddenly we're there, and he's got the key card out, his other arm still holding me, supporting me.

Might I fall to the ground if he lets me go?

Most likely.

The door swings open and then we're inside, the room draped in darkness, the only light shining from the window facing the city street. The curtains cover most of the glass, only a sliver of fabric parted, but it lets in just enough light that I can see the grim determination on Cannon's face, the damp sheen of his swollen lips, his large hands as they reach out and cup my cheeks.

He clasps my head in his hands, his thumb drifting across my parted lips. I suck in a loud, shaky breath, my heart thudding wildly, my body taut with anticipation of what he might do next.

"You're so damn beautiful," he whispers just before he rests his mouth upon mine. My eyes slide closed, savoring the sensation of his lips against mine. This kiss is restrained. Explorative, but careful.

He still cradles my face, his tongue doing a slow, delicious search, and I simply...melt. Brain cells bleed together, my still-rapidly beating heart seems to dissolve, as do my bones and my muscles and my blood. Until I'm a languid heap draped over him, my fingers curled into his shirt fabric once more, like he's an anchor and I'm about to sink into endless black depths if I let him go.

My thoughts are chaos. Bordering on dramatic. Intuition kicks in, reminding me that I want to explore and touch and so I do. I let my hands slide up, fingers curling around his broad shoulders and squeezing just before they slide back down, drifting along the buttons of his shirt, brushing against his flat stomach. Feeling greedy, I slip two fingers between the buttons, barely touching his actual skin, and he shudders.

Power filters through me, solidifying what turned to liquid only moments before. He's still kissing me, his hands still cupping my face, and my trembling fingers undo one shirt button. Then another. And another and another until I've undone his entire shirt and my eager hands push the fabric aside. I break the kiss and step out of his hold so I can stare at the masculine beauty that is Cannon Whittaker's chest.

And it is a sight to behold. He's large and firm and there are muscles *everywhere*. His stomach is flat and ridged. There's dark hair curling across his pecs, a line of it starting just below his navel and disappearing into his trousers.

My mouth waters. I want to trace that trail with my fingers. Slip my hand beneath his trousers and see what I could find—

"You're starin' at me like you want to eat me up."

His rough voice startles me and I glance up at him, see the matching hunger that's driving me in his eyes too. "I think I do," I tell him, immediately wanting to roll my eyes at myself. "Want to eat you up."

He laughs. Shakes his head. Reaching for me, his hands are at my waist before he spins me around so my back is to him. He steps closer, pressing his body against mine, and I can feel him, heavy and hard, nestled against my backside.

I stare at the wall ahead of me, gulping. I want this. I do. But I'm realizing that once I commit to tonight, there's no turning back. As in, I'm going for it.

What will happen tomorrow? And the next day? And the day after that? He'll leave, and I'll still be here.

Alone.

"I wanna take this off," he whispers close to my ear, his fingers playing with the zip at the top of my dress. "Will you let me, Lady Susanna?"

I smile despite my nerves and worry. Calling me Lady Susanna at a time like this is amusing. No man I know would say it. Only the brash American would think it funny. And it is funny.

Sexy.

He steps away from me and I immediately miss his close-ness. His heat. He's quiet, and I wonder if he's waiting for me to answer.

Bending my head down, I brush my hair to the right, putting the back of my dress on display. Hopefully he'll know what I want without having to say a word.

SEVEN

CANNON

I DON'T KNOW what she wants.

Damn it, I've never been good at reading a woman's mind. What guy is any good at it? I know married men, guys who are fucking happy as shit in their relationships, and they complain that they're not mind readers and that sometimes they don't know what their woman wants from them. They always sound helpless as shit about it too.

So of course, at this very important moment in time, I'm clueless.

But the longer she stands there silently before me, like an offering, the quicker I figure out what she's doing. The zipper is on full display and I reach out and grab it, undoing it with shaky fingers.

The fabric parts slowly, revealing her smooth skin, her nude-colored bra. The zipper stops at the base of her spine, and I catch a glimpse of lacy panties.

Just like that, I'm hard.

Truthfully, I've been hard for about the last hour, but now I'm well and truly popping a tent in my pants.

"I must confess something."

Her soft voice reaches me seconds after she said the actual words, and I blink myself back into focus. "What's up?"

She turns her head, glancing at me from over her shoulder, her lips curved. I can definitely tell her what's up. All she's gotta do is look at my dick and see. He is up and ready for action. "I'm not wearing sexy underwear."

I check out the back of her bra again. Looks pretty standard. My gaze drops to where the zipper dangles, right above a lacy waistband. "I might have to argue with you."

"No, it's true." She turns to face me, the dress crumpling forward, revealing the tops of her shoulders. They're slender and smooth and I want to kiss them. "My bra is— industrial strength."

I'm confused. Frowning. "Say what?"

"I have." She pauses. Shrugs, her cheeks coloring. "Rather large breasts. And so I always tend to—restrain them."

Well, that's a damn shame. I'm tempted to tell her that, but I can see this conversation pains her, and I don't to make this any more embarrassing, so instead, I reach for her. Pull her into my arms so she's snug against me, her body fitting to mine like a just-found piece to my life puzzle.

Whoa, getting ahead of yourself there.

"Can I see them?" I ask her as I study her face. She's so damn pretty. Skin smooth and pink, eyes blue as the sky and a pert little nose. There's a hint of curl around her hairline, and I wonder if this straight hair thing she's got going on isn't natural.

I like the idea of her hair being curly. Wild.

She wrinkles her nose. "This is the strangest pre-sex conversation I've ever had."

My blood turns hot at her words. "What you're telling me is we're going to have sex?" I remind myself not to get my hopes up too high, but she did say *pre*-sex, so...

"Isn't that what we're leading up to?"

"Yeah." I briefly kiss her, and when I pull away, her lips follow after mine, like she doesn't want to stop. "That's what I'm hoping for."

"Right." She touches my chest, her fingers branding my bare skin. "Same here."

"Are you sure?" Again with the asking. But I'm not going to push her into anything she doesn't want to do. She has to know the score. This is meaningless.

Just fun.

No strings.

"So sure," she murmurs just before she leans in and presses her damp lips to my chest. That first touch is like a jolt of electricity to my junk, and when she keeps kissing me, her tongue darting out to lick my nipple, well fuck.

A man can restrain himself for only so long.

I grab hold of her and pick her up, carrying her over to the bed. She's a squealing, squirming woman in my arms, her constant movement causing her dress to become looser and looser, and when I basically toss her onto the bed, the sleeves fall completely off her arms, leaving her bare above the waist except for the bra.

And she's not wrong when she described it as industrial. That sucker is holding her breasts in so well, I can hardly see them. Just a hint of cleavage. Smooth, creamy skin.

My fingers are itching to touch her there.

I join her on the bed and kiss her, one hand on her cheek, the other moving to her back, fingers fumbling with the bra clasp. It takes a couple of attempts—her tongue in my mouth is a total distraction—but I finally undo it. She's so caught up in the kiss, she doesn't seem to notice when I push the straps from her shoulders, helping them slide down until they're at her elbows. And when I break the kiss and pull away from her, she keeps her eyes closed while I take her bra completely off and toss it onto the floor.

Her eyes fly open as realization sets in, one arm shifting to cover her abundant chest. But all she manages to do is cover her nipples and plump her breasts up, making them look even bigger.

And sexier.

"Stop," I tell her, gently removing her arm away from her chest and then pressing two fingers against her shoulder. "Lay down."

She does as I ask, her eyes never leaving mine as she slowly lowers her head onto the pillow. Her breasts are full and lush and topped with perfectly pink, perfectly hard nipples. Her dress is now bunched up around her waist, and I reach for the fabric and tug down, quickly removing the dress so she's lying before me in a pair of lacy cream-colored panties and nothing else.

"You look pretty fuckin' sexy to me," I tell her as I sweep my hands along the sides of her legs, my fingers sliding over her thighs until I'm pushing them apart. "I like your panties."

"Cannon," she says, as if I'm in trouble, but her voice is too shaky and breathless for me to take her seriously.

She likes what I'm saying. And how I'm touching her.

"Whatcha got under here?" I ask as my fingers toy with the side of her underwear. The fabric is thin. I could tear those panties right off her without any trouble, but I don't want to scare the woman.

"I think you know what I've got under there," she says, a full body shudder overtaking her when I slip my fingers inside and encounter pubic hair.

"Hmm, I think I'll wait." I remove my hand from her panties and shift over her, dropping my head to her chest. I kiss her there, pressing my lips to the center where I can feel her wildly beating heart. I turn my attention to one breast, kissing and licking, nibbling her skin while I caress her other breast with busy fingers. Circling and circling, making that nipple extra hard while I continue to kiss and lick her right breast.

"Oh God," she gasps when I draw her nipple into my mouth and give it a firm pull. I pinch the other nipple while I continue to suck and she bucks beneath me, as if I've shocked her. I trade off to the other nipple, sucking and pinching, licking and biting. She's clawing at my back, her nails sharp even through the fabric of my shirt, and I yank away from her, shoving my shirt off so it falls onto the floor.

I press her into the mattress, covering her entire body with mine, my hips between her thighs, my bare chest against hers. My mouth finds hers and we kiss wildly with tongues and teeth, her moans already driving me to the brink. I touch her everywhere I can reach and she does the same, those fluttering hands hovering over my dick. Unable to help myself, I press against her palm, give her exactly what she's been seeking, and when she starts stroking me, I swear to fucking God, I see stars.

"Not gonna come that way," I tell her, the words falling between her lips as we continue to kiss.

"I want you to come inside me," she whispers back, her bold words driving me on.

Though she better mean come inside her while I'm wearing a condom...

One more long, languid kiss and then I'm off the bed, kicking off my stupid shoes, shucking my pants and under-wear to the floor. I then have to grab them again to pull my wallet out, flipping it open to find the single condom I leave in there for moments just like this.

These sorts of moments were a lot more frequent when I first started playing for the NFL. Back when I'd fuck anything with a willing pussy.

Sounds trashy as hell, but all the single players do it, and even some of the committed ones do too. We're young and rich and hoping to be richer and seeking celebrity status.

Women come running, spreading their legs easily. Part their lips easily too.

It was a whirlwind of sex with strangers, and I was over it a while ago.

So what's with me and Susanna tonight? She's pretty much a stranger, and we're about to have sex. It shouldn't feel any different from my previous experiences with football groupies and the hot, readily available women looking for a good time and a quick fuck.

I can't group Susanna with any of those women, though. She's...different. Which sounds corny as hell, I know this, but I can't help but think that it's true.

Susanna is definitely different.

"Oh my goodness."

Her startled voice knocks me from my thoughts and I realize quick she's sitting in the middle of the mattress, staring at my naked body. I'm still standing next to the bed, condom in hand, cock jutting out toward her like it's waving hello.

I'll be inside you soon, can't wait.

"You all right?" I ask as I frown at her.

Her eyes never stray from my dick. "You're...*massive.*"

I chuckle. "I'm pretty big everywhere."

"What size shoe do you wear?"

Say what? "Sixteen."

She blinks up at me. "What...oh, that's right. You Americans have different shoe sizes."

Huh. I had no idea that was a thing. "Trust me. A sixteen is big, Susanna."

"I assumed."

"I've measured my dick before too." I grab hold of my erection and give it a firm stroke, her gaze never straying from my hand. "Want to know the length?"

She hurriedly shakes her head. "I'm afraid you might scare me more if you give me facts and figures."

"Jesus, woman, don't be scared." I rejoin her on the bed, crawling over her and grabbing her arms. I lift them up, gently pinning them above her head to the mattress, my gaze on hers. "I'll fit."

Her eyebrows wrinkle in seeming concern. "Don't be too sure about that."

If this mean she's extra tight, I will probably bust my nut before I barely get inside her. "I'll make sure you're nice and wet."

Her mouth falls open. "You...will?"

"Oh yeah." She seems surprised that I said that. "Isn't that what I'm supposed to do?"

"Well, yes. Of course. I just..." Her voice drifts and I dip my head, brushing my mouth against hers.

"You just what?" I murmr.

"I've never had a man tell me that he'll—take care of me. In bed," she admits.

"You're not used to talkers then." I have a reputation as a guy who doesn't say much. I don't talk to the media very often, if it all. I don't say a lot of bullshit when I'm being interviewed by anyone—and I rarely get interviewed by anyone because of that.

But when I'm intimate with a woman? For some reason, I'm a talker, and it always surprises them.

Always.

"Not particularly, no," she admits.

"Does it embarrass you? My talking?" I ask before I lean in and rest my mouth against her throat. I nip her. Give her a little lick. "Fuck, you taste good," I mutter.

A little whimper escapes her. "It's not embarrassing, no."

"You won't mind then, if I talk about eating your juicy pussy?" I lift away from her to catch her reaction.

She slaps her hands over her face, a laugh escaping her as she spreads her fingers wide so I can see her eyes peeking through. They dance with amusement. And arousal. "God, Cannon, really? My juicy—*pussy?*" She chokes out that last word, which makes me laugh too.

"I bet it's real wet," I tell her after my laughter dies, my hand wandering across her soft belly, fingers slipping beneath the waistband of her panties. "I bet I can make it even wetter."

Her legs go wider, and I know she wants me to make that pussy wetter.

I will happily oblige.

EIGHT

SUSANNA

CANNON HAS A VERY determined expression on his face. His lips are thin, his gaze steely and his jaw extra firm. Even his nostrils are flaring, and I never thought that to be particularly sexy on a man, but on Cannon...

That would be a yes.

All his talk about making my—pussy (yes, I'm having a hard time even thinking the word, though I did actually say it out loud only a few moments ago) wetter, is indeed making it wetter. And now that he's sliding my panties off with those big hands of his, his fingers brushing against my legs on purpose, my entire body is trembling in anticipation of what he might do next.

He surprises me by dropping soft kisses across my stomach. Gentle, damp touches of his lips, no licking tongue or sharp teeth involved. My eyes tightly closed, I try to calm my ragged breathing, pretend that I've got it together. That this is no big deal, being in this giant man's bed, his hands all over my naked body. But it's so very difficult when I can't stop thinking about the insistent pulsing between my legs.

And how Cannon's face will most likely end up between my legs.

All of his soft, sweet kisses are a tease. His fingers tickle the inside of my thighs. His tongue dips into my bellybutton, making me inhale sharply at the shock of it. Those giant hands of his push my legs open as he readjusts his position between my thighs and then...

And then.

His mouth is there. A teasing brush. A quick kiss, an exhalation of hot breath upon my most sensitive skin. I squirm beneath him, wanting more, unsure of how I should ask, frantically trying to come up with ways to ask.

He's driving me absolutely insane, and he really hasn't even done anything yet.

Cannon pulls away and remains still, like he's studying me down there, and I crack open my eyes to find that yes indeed, he is definitely studying me down there.

"I like that you're not waxed," he observes, his gaze never leaving my most intimate spot.

I frown at him. "What do you mean?" I trim it a bit, shave a little here and there, but I don't go completely bare. Considering the men in my life are pretty few and far between at the moment, what's the point in getting a complete wax job only to end up itchy and miserable when it grows back in?

Not like anyone's checking me out down there anyway lately.

Not until Cannon.

"You've got a pretty full bush." He actually finger combs my "pretty full bush," and I must admit, it feels...wonderful. Though anytime Cannon touches me, it feels wonderful. "I like it."

"Um, thank you," I say weakly, because I don't know how else to answer him.

"You're welcome," he says with a chuckle, his mouth hovering just above where I want him the most. "You're extra pretty down here too."

I've never had a man compliment my vagina before. Should I find this rather odd? Because for some reason, I don't. "You think so?"

"Oh yeah. All pink and glistening." He dips his head and licks me with his wide tongue, shocking a loud gasp out of me. "You taste good too."

I'm about to say something else, something completely inane and silly, but then he starts licking me in earnest, his tongue everywhere at once, his fingers spreading me wide as he sets his focus on my clitoris. He licks and sucks it greedily, drawing the bit of flesh between his lips, slipping one finger, then another inside of me.

It takes no time at all for my orgasm to draw closer, hovering just beyond the horizon, and I swear I'm about to fall over that delicious edge when he pulls away and asks, "You like that?"

My fingers curl into fists and I pound the mattress with frustration. "I freaking love it."

I never, absolutely ever say things like *I freaking love it.*

What is this man doing to me?

He laughs and I glance down, our gazes connecting. He's lying on his stomach, elbows propped, face right between my legs. We watch each other silently, my breath stalling in my throat when he lowers his head, his gaze still never leaving mine as he slowly licks me. I sink my teeth into my lower lip, my chest tight as I continue to hold my breath, unable to look away as he laps at my flesh like I'm an ice-cold popsicle on a steaming hot day.

It's too much, watching him and feeling what he's doing to me at the same time. I swear I'm getting lightheaded, and I realize it's because I'm still holding my breath.

Exhaling loudly, I lean my head back and close my eyes.

He stops what he's doing. Doesn't say a word, doesn't touch me, just...stops.

"What's wrong?" I breathe.

"You need to watch me." His voice is deep and dark, the words like a command.

"I don't know if I can stand it," I admit, my eyes still closed.

"You won't get what you want if you don't watch," he says.

My eyes pop open and I lift my head, our gazes meeting once again. His lips are shiny, his eyes dark, his hair a mess, and all I can think about is, how fast can he put his mouth and tongue back on me?

"Don't look away," he whispers as he ducks his head once more, his tongue flickering against my clit.

It's much more intense, watching a man go down on you. Most of my encounters with this particular activity are done in the dark. My first boyfriend had become quite excellent at it because it was all he wanted to do, and I was a willing participant. The other occasions with men going down on me had mostly been a disappointment. They never managed to find the right parts to focus on, and I was too chicken to direct them where they needed to be.

That was my own fault, and it's a problem I still have now. I'm not the most vocal or demanding in bed. After a while, I figured I'd become spoiled by my first, overeager boyfriend. No one was as good as Colin. That boy gave me multiple orgasms.

Multiple.

But Colin has met his match, and his name is Cannon. The man knows exactly where to zero in on, and my entire body is singing with the potential to orgasm at any given moment. I'm trying my best to think of other things just to draw this moment out. Like how I need to do my washing and give my tiny place a good dusting.

All thoughts of cleaning my flat are gone. All I can focus on is the intense sensations that are slowly taking me over. He keeps flicking his tongue, increasing the speed, his fingers sliding inside my body, back and forth. In and out. I'm shaking. He presses his tongue flat against my clit, does this unusual pulsing thing that I've never felt before in my life, and then I'm shouting.

Shouting.

And coming. Oh God, I'm coming and coming, my entire body convulsing as if I have no control over it, and Cannon is gripping my hip in one hand, two fingers from his other hand curled deep inside my body, touching some magical place that's making me convulse even harder.

It's so overwhelming, I'm seeing spots. Like I might actually black out from an orgasm.

Who knew?

Seconds later—possibly minutes, maybe even hours—Cannon slides his body up so he's lying beside me, his heavy arm flung across my stomach, his mouth seeking mine. I let him kiss me, so exhausted I can barely move. I taste myself on his lips, on his tongue, and it's strangely arousing.

So of course I do manage to kiss him back and then he's slapping his hand all over the mattress, searching for the forgotten condom, and I find it first, placing it in his hand without a word. No words are needed, we know what we want. He rises up on his knees, his erection jutting out toward me, the tip glistening with a single drop of creamy liquid, and unable to stop myself, I lean up and flick my tongue across the head of his cock.

"Jesus," he breathes out, his expression telling me I've just blown his mind. I'll blow him more if he lets me. "Do that again."

I do it again, rising up on my elbows and opening my mouth, letting him slip his erection between my lips. I suck and lick just the head, my gaze lifting to meet his as he watches me with complete and utter fascination.

Again, I'm not big on the blowjob thing. I gave Colin plenty of them because I wanted to return the favor and we were both young and experimental and ready to do it all. Of.

The. Time. There is nothing more exhilarating as young love. First love.

This, though, is completely intoxicating. He's watching me, and I'm watching him, and his long, thick cock is in my mouth, and I'm...loving it. Oral sex on the first date is not my thing, but I get the sense that this entire night isn't going the way it usually does.

And I'm okay with it.

"We gotta stop." He pulls his erection from my mouth, his expression, his voice full of agonizing torture. "I can't do this."

I'm disappointed he's gone. "Why not?"

"I won't come in your mouth."

"But I came in your mouth," I point out, shocked by my words. I'm exploring new territory tonight.

"I know, and it was fucking amazing, but I don't want to blow my entire wad and be done with it." He blinks at me, and apparently now he's sleepy, his eyes are so heavy lidded. I wonder if he's still suffering from a major case of jet lag. "I want to fuck you so I can feel your pussy squeeze all the come out of me."

Oh. My.

His words are incredibly rude. At least, that's what I'm telling myself.

So why am I attacking him like an uncontrollable, sex-deprived demon? I practically throw myself at him, my mouth finding and fusing with his, my hands roaming, my lower body grinding against his erection.

God, he feels so good. So incredibly hard and firm and manly. He's sweaty and grunting and it all feels so primal. So crude and base and raw and wonderful.

He lets me act like a sex maniac for all of about two minutes and then he takes complete control of the situation, flipping us over so my back is on the mattress and he's above me. Somehow in the chaos he rolled the condom onto his cock, and I watch in fascination as he rises up on his knees again, grabs hold of my hip with one hand and the base of his erection with the other, and slowly brushes the tip against me.

I'm shivering just at that first touch. I'm so wet, I can actually hear the, ahem, juicy sounds my flesh is making, and he's smiling. So wide, I know exactly what he's thinking.

"See? Your pussy is juicy," he says, sounding proud.

Oh my.

I knew he would say that.

"It won't hurt," he tells me, his voice low and even as he slowly pushes himself inside me. I immediately tense up. "Breathe." I do as he says, willing myself to relax. "Nope, it won't hurt. Not a bit. Just relax, baby, and I'll make you feel good."

His words should sound cheesy. If I read them in a romance novel, I'd probably roll my eyes, and I love the occasional romance novel.

But I am so thoroughly enjoying the way he speaks to me, and maybe that's because no other man has even attempted such naughty talk. They don't talk about blowing wads and squeezing come and juicy pussies and oh my God, he just slipped all the way inside me and I feel so incredibly *full*.

He pauses, waiting, his breathing harsh. I open my eyes to find him hovering above me, his eyes closed, sweat dripping down the side of his face. Again, the ick factor should be on high alert for me right now—normally I'm not a fan of sweat —but I'm tempted to rub myself all over him so I can get just as sweaty as he is.

Clearly, I have a problem.

"Why aren't you—doing anything?" I ask after a long quiet moment.

"I'm trying to keep my shit under control," he says through clenched teeth.

"What do you mean?" I'm a little confused.

"I'm afraid if I start moving, I'll unleash on you, and it'll be over in two seconds," he confesses, the pain on his face obvious. "And I don't wanna do that."

I want him to do that. I want to see this man unleash on me. I'm sure it would be amazing.

"Just...move slow," I suggest, wiggling my hips, sending him somehow even deeper, and we both groan at the sensation.

"I don't know if I'm gonna be able to move slow with you, Susie. And that's a fact."

My heart warms at him calling me Susie. No one has ever really called me that before. Even when I was a small child, my parents always called me Susanna. Never Susie or Anna or any type of nickname, beyond the occasional *darling* or *sweetheart*.

I grew up in a very formal house, and while silly nicknames were popular amongst all of my friends' households, they weren't in my house.

And that made me sad.

So Cannon calling me Susie touches my heart more than it probably should, but I can't help it.

I sort of love it.

"Then move fast," I whisper encouragingly. "Unleash on me. I don't care if it's over in two seconds."

"I want it to last longer," he says as he starts to move his hips. He pulls almost all the way out before pushing himself back in, a slow, delicious drag of hard, hot flesh that has my toes curling. "Fuck, there is no way I can make this last longer."

With those words, he does as he predicted and unleashes on me. His hips pump at maximum speed as he fucks me thoroughly. There is no other way to describe it. He fucks me like he was born to do it, his muscles straining, his chest heaving, his cock spearing in and out of my body, little grunts accompanied every thrust. All I can do is cling to him. Slip my legs around his waist to send him even deeper. Moan encouraging little sounds in his ear as I wrap my body around his. I can't come up with words, not yet, I'm still too...I don't know, shy, maybe?

But I can imagine that if we keep this up, if we keep seeing each other and having sex like this?

I'll be a dirty talking, blabbering idiot in no time.

NINE

CANNON

I WAKE up in the middle of the night to find a curvy woman wrapped completely around me. Her face his tucked into my neck, her arm draped across my chest, her leg thrown around mine. I pull her in closer, burying my face in her sweet-smelling hair, and the swell in my chest is an old, familiar feeling.

A feeling I can't have for this particular woman because we are definitely not meant to be.

Not many people know this about me, but I'm a fall-hard kind of man. Meaning, if I make a connection with a woman, I will fall completely head over heels for her.

Even if it fucks me up and is a complete disaster.

The first time it happened, I was in high school. Her name was Emily, but everyone called her Em. Rebellious and troubled, she was kind of a nightmare. But man, I loved that girl. She truly felt my faith and belief in her helped turned her rebellious behavior around. She graduated high school even though, at one point, everyone believed she'd fail or drop out. I went away to college on a mostly full scholarship while she stayed at home and attended the local community college near where we grew up.

And she stuck to that plan. We grew apart, though, and mutually split up within months of me going away to school. I was completely depressed for almost a solid year. She met another guy within two months of our breakup, and last I heard, she's still with him. And the funniest thing of all? She's a teacher.

She fucking tortured our teachers all through school and now she's one of them.

Em wasn't the only one I fell for. There were a couple of others. One named Mary, and oh my goddamn, did she about finish me off. Our senior year in college I was so fucking sprung over that girl, and she knew it. She cruelly smashed my heart to bits again and again, ending it with me only to come crawling back. And I took her back. Three times.

She about broke me.

That's the reason I gave up on relationships. I fall too hard, too fast. I'd rather keep it impersonal and have the occasional hookup, though even those don't appeal to me as much anymore.

But now...there's this woman wrapped all around me like she never wants to let go. Naked and smelling sweet and skin so damn soft, I can't stop from touching her.

I grope her lazily, my fingers playing with her full breasts, tweaking her nipples. My cock rises halfheartedly to the occasion, but I don't really think I want to fuck her. Not now.

I'm still too tired.

Minutes tick by, though, and I'm lying in bed wide awake, fucked up by the time change. Exhilarated from the outrageous sex we just had. Seeing that innocent face and those lush lips wrap tight around my cock? Yeah, talk about too much. This woman just about undoes me.

The weirdest part? I don't even know her.

Not really.

"Mmm." She rustles against me, her fragrant hair brushing my face, her foot brushing against my calf. "You are so hairy."

"What?" I'm chuckling. What a random thing to say.

"I don't normally like hairy men," she continues, her lips brushing against my chest as she talks. "But I like you."

"I'm not that hairy, Susie."

"Oh, but you are." She lifts her head, her sleepy gaze meeting mine. Her hair is a tousled mess, her lips are swollen and she has razor burn on her cheeks, all because of me. "Your chest is hairy." She touches the hair there to prove her point. "And your legs are super hairy."

"Kind of like your bush?" I reach down and play with it, and she slaps my arm.

"You say the rudest things," she accuses, but she doesn't sound that mad about it.

"You like it."

"Hmm. I might." She takes a deep breath as she rolls away from me and grabs her phone from the bedside table where she must've left it. I don't remember her doing that. "It's three in the morning."

"Can't sleep."

She looks at me. "Oh. Is it the time difference?" When I nod my answer, she says, "That must be so—difficult."

"It is," I say with a sigh. She rolls over on her side again, her back to me, the sheet having fallen down and putting her magnificent ass on full display. Unable to help myself, I reach out and give it a gentle slap.

"Hey!" She turns to face me, her expression full of shock. "You slapped me."

"You don't like a little ass play?" I ask innocently.

"Ass play?"

Those two words said in her elegant British accent is kind of a turn on, I'm not gonna lie. "Yeah, ass play. I'm guessing you've never done anything like that?"

"What exactly are you talking about?" she asks slowly, her gaze...

Curious.

Hot damn.

I bet if I play this right, I can indulge in a little more ass play with Lady Susanna.

"Nothing too crazy. A little slap here and there, nothing too painful, but just enough to sting. A finger inserted. Maybe some anal sex," I explain, trying to keep it casual.

She blinks at me. We never did close the curtain, so there's some light in the room. Just enough so I can make out her beautiful features, and see her voluptuous body. She has a body that's made to fuck, and I know that makes me sound like a complete asshole, but it's true. Her body is curvy, sexy perfection.

And despite the fact I have to get up in a few hours and play football on international television, my cock is on high alert, and I'm ready for more.

"I've never done...anything like that before," she says, her big blue eyes extra luminous in the light.

"Do you want to?"

Susanna presses her lips together.

"If not, no big deal," I tell her.

She shifts toward me quietly, pushing at my shoulders so I'm flat on my back. She crawls up the length of my body, dragging that lush body across mine until her tits are crushed against my chest and she fits all snug and perfect to me. "I'm willing to try just about anything with you," she says just before she kisses me.

It's a delicious kiss, full of sighs and whispery moans and searching tongues. My hands wander, as usual, smoothing up and down, over her ass. She spreads her legs wider, so they fall over my hips and she's straddling me.

Leaving herself completely open.

But I don't touch her there. Not yet. I gotta lead up to this. Instead, I keep stroking her ass. I stroke her pussy too, and find it wet and creamy and hot as fucking fire. My cock lets me know it wants in, like soon, and I tell it to wait.

I have other things to take care of first.

Shit, and then there's the fact that I don't have any more condoms...

"Roll over, baby," I tell her, and she does it without protest, lying on the mattress for me, spread eagle with every inch of her on display. Her pussy is wide open and ready for me so I dive down and give it a lick, my tongue playing with her clit, making her shudder and squirm beneath me, her hands going to my hair, tugging and pulling and making me wince.

Yet I don't stop. It's like I can't let up.

I want her coming all over my lips.

"I need you inside me," she whispers, and I lift my head to study her, regret crashing down on me, knowing what I have to say.

"No can do, baby. I don't have any more condoms," I tell her.

"What?" she practically screeches, her eyes wide. She lets go of my hair, the disappointment written all over her.

"I only had the one from my wallet."

"This—this won't do." She leaps out of bed and flicks on the lamp, making me blink against the harsh yellow light that fills the room. "They might have a box somewhere in this room, right? This is a high-end hotel."

"And high-end hotels don't usually provide their guests with condoms," I say with a chuckle. Not the ones I stay at, at least.

"You never know." She goes into the bathroom and I hear drawers being opened and closed, mysterious things clacking and dropping, a few whispered curses.

This girl is fiery when she's determined, which is totally unexpected.

The bathroom light shuts off and then she's standing next to the bed, the room phone in her hand, and when the operator answers, she starts talking.

"Yes, I was wondering if it would be possible to have a box of condoms delivered to Mister Cannon Whittaker's room?" She pauses as the person on the line speaks, and I sit up in bed, shocked at what she's saying. "Yes, I know it's three in the morning, but it's rather—important." Another pause, then she smiles. "You'll send them up in fifteen minutes? Lovely. Thank you very much."

Susanna hangs up the phone, looking rather pleased with herself. "We'll have condoms in fifteen minutes."

"Damn, woman, that was sexy," I tell her, crawling out of bed so I can grab hold of her. But she's a slippery thing, and she's keeping me on my toes. The moment I reach for her, she yelps and starts running around the room like a crazy woman, buck-naked with her hair flying and her tits bouncing. I do what any hot-blooded man would do and chase after her, catching her when I get her cornered near the door, a triumphant smile on my face when she realizes she's stuck. I grab hold of her wrists with one hand and pin her, my cock like an insistent third friend between us.

"Gotcha," I whisper, my face drawing closer to hers.

"I might get away," she threatens, and I laugh.

"You can't. I got you." I kiss her, trying to drug her with my lips, and of course, it works. She's returning my kiss with gusto, and I keep my hold on her wrists as I break the kiss and drop to my knees, my mouth landing on her pussy.

We're like that long minutes later, two orgasms in, her legs shaking, her throat hoarse from her screams. My face is covered in come, and when there's a knock on the door, I pull away from her, both of us wide-eyed.

"Hello! Package for Mister Whittaker!"

"Shit," I mutter as I rise to my feet, scrubbing my hand across my face. My dick is sticking straight out like a pole, and should I mention just how big it is?

Because it's big. And obvious.

"Get a robe on," Susanna suggests in a hushed whisper just before she runs to the bathroom.

"With my dick sticking out of it as I open the door? I don't think so," I mutter.

The knock sounds again. "Mister Whittaker? Are you in there?"

"Give me a minute!" I yell back, wincing at the sound of my agitated voice.

I'm such an asshole.

"Here." Susanna exits the bathroom, wearing a white hotel robe and clutching another one in her hands. "Wear this and answer the door."

I take the robe from her, letting my gaze run over her. "You answer the door."

"What?" She rests a hand against her chest. "No. I couldn't possibly."

"Why not?"

"They'll know what I've been doing," she says, her voice squeaky.

"Yeah, well, they'll figure out what I'm going to do here in a minute, even if they weren't delivering condoms." I drop my gaze to my dick, which is still thrusting straight out.

Susanna covers her mouth, smothering a giggle. "I can't answer the door like this. I look like I've been..."

"Thoroughly fucked? Yes, you do." I lean in and drop a tender kiss to her lips before pulling away. "But it's okay. You'll never see this person again."

She looks doubtful. "I don't know."

"Then I guess we won't get the condoms."

Determination crossing her features, she shoves me into the bathroom, runs a hand over her wild hair and then unlocks and opens the door. "Hello," she says breathlessly, clutching the front of the robe to her.

"Good morning." The man in the suit isn't that much older than either of us, and he's not bad looking either. He's eyeing Susanna with undisguised interest, the rat bastard. "Is Mister Whittaker available?" he asks.

"He's—predisposed at the moment, but I can take the delivery." Her cheery voice can almost make me forget I had her pinned to the wall and my mouth on her pussy only a few minutes ago.

I watch as she holds out her hand and the man slaps the box of condoms in her palm.

I gotta give it to her, Susanna keeps her composure while accepting those condoms. I'd never know she was frazzled or embarrassed. The only thing giving her away is the pink in her cheeks.

"Thank you very much," she tells the man as she starts to shut the door.

"Have a wonderful morning," he tells her just as the door closes.

I need to remember to somehow give that guy a large tip for his discretion.

"Ha, we will," I say as I exit the bathroom, grab hold of Susanna's waist and haul her over to the bed.

Where I show her all the ways I can make her morning wonderful.

TEN

SUSANNA

I'M EXHAUSTED. I barely got any sleep, yet I've never felt more alive.

"I want you to come to the game," Cannon says yet again, after I've already turned him down. Twice. "Come on, Susie. Say yes."

"Cannon. I wouldn't understand what I'm watching. I know nothing about American football," I protest, though that's not the real reason I don't want to go.

Cutting him off is smart. We had our fun, and now it's over. Going to his game would just draw this entire situation out.

"I can explain it to you real quick," he says, and I shake my head firmly.

"No, you really can't. You need to take a shower and leave." I sound like a mother, but it's true. He has to go soon and we've already wasted so much time.

Not that I view my time with Cannon as a waste. It's been magical, really. My entire body aches in places I didn't know could hurt.

"Take a shower with me and I'll explain it all in there," he says, his voice, his face so hopeful, he looks like a young boy.

He's no young boy, though. Not with the way he touched me last night and this morning. I've lost count of how many orgasms I've had.

Lost. Count.

That's just...insane.

"If we take a shower together, that will lead to other things," I say primly, glancing down at my chest. I'm wearing one of his T-shirts—and my plan is to keep it forever—so at least I'm not completely naked. And Cannon is walking around the room in a pair of black boxer briefs and nothing else.

Leaving his chest and abs on perfect display, and I can't stop staring.

"Come on, Susanna. I really want you there. Just say yes." He stands at the foot of the bed, his arms crossed, biceps bulging.

"You're being ridiculous," I say with a sigh, my gaze straying to his biceps. I want to touch them. Feel those strong arms wrap around me again...

"I'm stubborn. It's an important thing you should know about me. When I want something, I won't take no for an answer." He raises a single brow, something I wish I could do, but I've never been able to manage it.

He's sooo bloody frustrating.

"I should go home," I start, but he cuts me off.

"Yeah, you should. Go home, change into something more comfortable, and go to the game. I'll leave your name everywhere, leave you a ticket at will call, whatever I've got to do to get you in there. Just please, Susanna." He sends me puppy dog eyes, his lips formed in a cute little pout. "Come to my game."

I roll my eyes. Make an irritated noise. "Fine." I throw my arms into the air. "I'll go."

He tackles me. Throws himself onto the bed and takes me down with him. Though the entire move is gentle. He doesn't hurt me. More like the move is protective as he cradles me in between those thick arms.

"Thank you for agreeing," he says, his voice sincere, his gaze boring into mine. "I'm glad you'll be there. Let's do something together after the game, too."

"I'm not—"

He steals the rest of my words with kiss, and I give in.

———

I'm DIGGING through the tiny wardrobe in my tiny flat, lamenting over my lack of anything casual yet pretty, when my phone rings. Considering it's under a pile of jumpers in various shades of gray, I'm surprised it's still ringing when I finally find it.

"I've done something, and I'm afraid you'll think me totally mad," I answer as I go through my gray jumpers once again.

"Please tell me what you've done. I need to focus on someone else's drama for once in my life," says my best friend, Evie.

We've known each other forever. Our fathers are close friends too.

"You won't believe it if I told you." I glance at the clock on the wall and see that I have maybe an hour before I need to leave. Thank goodness I've already taken a shower, and hopefully traffic won't be too dreadful.

But it probably will be. It'll take me forever to get there, to find parking—because I currently have my father's old Mercedes, so why not drive it?—and when I finally do make it to the stadium, most of the game will be over and I'll have to fake it to Cannon that I saw the entire game.

"Give it a try. I'd love to hear what you consider a wild story." Evie's tone is dry, edged with sarcasm, and that's because she loves to give me a hard time about being... boring. Not in a mean way, it's just facts. She's the wild child in our friendship. The one who's drawn to rebellious men, who can't keep a job even though she really doesn't need to, considering how wealthy her family is. Over the years she's dyed her hair a variety of colors, pierced her nose, her bellybutton and some part of her vagina I told her I didn't want to know about, and she has secret tattoos.

They're secret because she knows her parents will have coronaries if they ever found out about them.

"Are you sure you want to hear this?" I'm teasing her. Drawing this out. But I need to get on with it.

Time is limited.

"Jesus, just tell me already."

"I met a man last night. And...I slept with him."

Evie's quiet for a moment. "Did you actually sleep with him or have *sex* with him?"

"I had sex with him," I say quietly. "Many times."

"How many times?"

"I...lost count."

Evie whistles low. "Seriously? Was he any good? What am I asking, he had to be good. You lost count."

"He was the best I've ever had," I confess.

"Better than Colin?" She knows I judge all dates by Colin standards.

"*Much* better," I say with emphasis. "In every way better than Colin, if you understand what I'm saying."

"Whoa, so are you telling me you found someone who's better at going down on a woman than *Colin?*" Even Evie thinks Colin is the king of lady head. She's heard all the stories, all the lurid details. We share everything, Evie and I.

"Yes," I say eagerly, wishing I could go into more detail.

Or...hmm. Maybe not. Maybe I shouldn't go into full detail about last night. What happened between Cannon and me should be private.

Sacred.

"Please tell me who is this man with the magical mouth?" Evie asks.

"He has a magical dick too." There goes my plan on keeping my moment with Cannon private and sacred.

"Seriously? I'm so jealous, darling. I haven't had good dick since I don't know when," Evie gushes. She's called herself a connoisseur of dick before, so I guess she should know.

"He's also very sweet." I think of all the nice gestures he made last night. He was a gentleman, yet a complete pervert too. It was an intoxicating mixture, I can't deny it.

"Who is this unicorn of a man?"

"Here's the thing. He's a footballer."

"Oh God. You know I've had a few of those," she says, sounding completely horrified.

"An American footballer," I add.

"*Oh.*" Now she sounds intrigued. "Is he one of those blokes who's over here for the exhibition game?"

"He is."

"What's his name?"

"Cannon Whittaker."

"What a name. Cannon. I'm looking him up on my iPad," Evie says.

"No, don't look him up!"

But it's too late. She finds him in seconds. I can tell by the way she goes quiet.

"I hate you. He's fucking beautiful!" Evie yells.

I pull the phone away from my ear with a wince. "He's attractive, yes."

"He's one big giant hunk of muscle," Evie says. "He's *massive.*"

"In every way you can think," I add.

"Oh, you smug bitch," Evie says with a laugh. "I can hear it in your voice. Clearly he gave you plenty of orgasms."

"So many," I say with a sigh, remembering the various ways he made them happen.

"I hate you so much."

"You already aid that. And more like you love me so much. Like I love you. Now I have to go, but I'll call you tomorrow. Maybe we can get together for brunch. Lunch. Dinner. Drinks. Something. Bye!"

I end the call before she can say anything else and grab a gray jumper, pulling it over my head and walking over to the mirror that hangs above my dresser. I have a serious thing for gray, clearly.

I smooth my hair down with my hand, frowning. I need to straighten it. If I don't, it gets too curly for my liking, especially when it's so damp outside, and I end up looking like a poodle.

After straightening my hair into submission, I find a hole in my jumper and I shuck it off, frustration making me groan aloud. My jeans—all three pairs of them—are either in the washing basket or don't fit me right. I can't go in leggings and a sweatshirt—I'll look like a bum off the street. And I can't wear a dress...

My gaze snags on yet another blue dress hanging in my wardrobe. With a sigh, I go to it, take the dress off the hanger, and slip it on. I turn this way and that, checking my reflection, and realize that it will do.

Perhaps he'll think I'm too stuffy, but there's nothing I can do about it now. I stand in my itty-bitty loo and apply mascara on my lashes, then slick on a pink shimmery lipgloss, all the while fighting my mental worry.

Last night with me wearing a dress and oh so formal with the Lady Susanna bit, he might've found me intriguing at first, but in his element, at a game, he'll see me for what I really am. A leftover debutante who works at an art gallery as a way to keep myself occupied while waiting to find a proper British gentleman to marry—one preferably with a title.

That is my parents' wish. That was my wish too, approximately two years ago, when I was twenty-one and increasingly desperate to get a ring on my finger. So many of my friends were already engaged, and I wanted that. At the very least, I wanted to be involved in a long-term relationship.

Whatever I could manage, I'd take it.

The relationship thing didn't happen for me, though. Two years later, and I'm still listless. Drifting in a sea of single people, yet not fully putting myself out there either. Part of the reason? I'm exhausted. I'm over it.

If it's supposed to happen, I'll meet the man of my dreams and it will all fall into place from there.

That's what's scary. Meeting Cannon last night felt down-right serendipitous. As if we were meant to be. The amazing connection, the sex, all of it seemed so...

Right.

Too right.

And that's frightening, when I consider the fact that the man doesn't even live here. He's not British. He's an American. A famous American celebrity football player who's probably only in it for the sex and that's it.

Don't go, the little voice inside my head whispers as I stare at my reflection in the bathroom mirror. *Stay home and clean up. Do your washing. Forget the brash American with the foul mouth.*

Ignoring the little voice, I exit the loo, grab my coat and my bag, and leave my flat. I don't want to forget the brash American with the foul mouth. I want to see him again.

I need to.

ELEVEN

CANNON

"I HEARD you have a new friend and she's waiting for you," Jordan says as we exit the locker room together.

"How the hell do you know that?" Even I wasn't sure if Susanna had made it to the game. By the time I got here, I barely had any time to change and get out on the field for practice. The coaches were pissed—I was the last one to arrive, and they gave me plenty of hell for it.

But last night with Susanna had been worth their anger.

"Mandy told me. She sent me a text," Jordan says, talking about his girlfriend. Well, ex-girlfriend. Possible current girlfriend. I'm still confused about their relationship status, but I'm glad she's back in his life. He smiles a lot more easily these days. "Said she's really sweet."

"She is." Her mouth is sweet. So is her pussy. Everything about Susanna is sweet as fucking heaven, but I can't really focus on that at the moment. "What's going on with you and Amanda anyway?"

"We're together." The possessive tone in Jordan's voice is a giveaway. I doubt he'll let Amanda go again, not like last time, when we were younger and, I guess, dumber. "Like we're supposed to be."

"I'm glad to hear it," I tell him, and it's true. Those two are made for each other, you can just tell. That whole destiny, fate thing that people say we can't avoid proves true for Jordan and Amanda.

And pondering my own destiny makes me reexamine my evening with Susanna. Were we meant to meet each other last night? Normally I think that sounds like a bunch of silly shit, but the connection I feel to this woman is so strong, I can't ignore it.

Or deny it.

As in, I'm currently dying to see her. Like anxious, jonesing-for-her-type behavior. I only do this when I fall hard, so I'm guessing I've...

Fallen hard.

Dangerous, right? I can't do this. I know I shouldn't. Yet here I am trying to control my pace as I walk beside Tuttle so I don't break out into a run in my search for Susanna.

"They're together right now. Amanda and Susanna. Waiting for us," Jordan says, and I barely hear him. My eyes are searching for her, my body tense in fear that maybe she already left.

Maybe she didn't want to see me after all.

But then I spot her. Standing next to Amanda just like Tuttle said she would be, looking as nervous as I feel, wearing a light blue dress that reminds me of the one she had on last night, and I can't help but wonder if she ever forgets her panties when she's wearing a dress.

I won't protest if she did. Easy access and all.

Jordan goes straight to Amanda and hugs and kisses her. I want to do the same, but the moment I get close to Susanna, she's giving off a weird vibe. She seems nervous. Agitated.

Uncomfortable even.

"Hey," I tell her, grabbing hold of her hand and pulling her in. Fuck it, she's getting a hug. But when I wrap my arms around her, she stiffens, and I release her immediately.

What the hell is going on?

"Hi." Her voice is shaky and she can barely meet my gaze. "You played wonderfully."

"Could you figure out what was happening?"

Her smile is faint. "Not particularly. But I still enjoyed it."

"Good." I scrub a hand along my jaw and she gives a little shrug.

I can't have this. We need a buffer tonight. "Yo, Tuttle." He doesn't hear me, so I clear my throat and speak louder. "What are your plans tonight?"

Jordan and Amanda turn to face us, and he frowns when he takes us in. "Not sure. All I know is I'm starving."

"Same," Amanda adds.

"All four of us should go to dinner," I suggest, slipping my arm around Susanna's shoulders and hauling her in close. I will wear her down, even if it takes me all night. "What do you think?"

"That sounds fantastic," Susanna says, staring up at me with adoring eyes, and the tension eases in my chest a bit.

"Yes, let's go to dinner. Have any suggestions, Susanna?" Amanda asks her.

Susanna nods with an enthusiastic grin. "Definitely. I can even drive us! I brought the family car."

The family car? I don't get it. She lives on her own yet drives the family car.

We walk out into the mostly empty parking lot, Susanna heading straight for an older, silver Mercedes.

"It's a beastly thing," she says as we approach it. "My father drove it as a teen, if you can even imagine. It's one of the safest cars on the road. That's why he insists I drive it."

"Protecting his baby girl?" I tease, reaching out and tugging on the ends of her hair.

Susanna darts away from me with a short yelp, a worried look suddenly crossing her face. "That and, well, I wasn't the best driver when I first started out."

Uh oh. "Maybe I should drive," I say, concern filling me.

"No, no. I know the roads far better than you ever could, and besides, you drive on the wrong side of the road." She waves a hand, offers up nervous laughter. "We'll be fine. Trust me."

I want to trust her. Actually, I *do* trust her.

The realization is wild. Eye opening. Mind bending.

And I don't know what to do about it. About...this.

Us.

Guess I'm just gonna go with it.

We all climb into the large sedan, and I feel like I can barely fit myself in the passenger seat. I really am a giant, especially in these European cars. I'm putting on my seatbelt when I notice Susanna reaching into a small compartment below the radio. She pulls out a pair of glasses and puts them on.

"My driving glasses," she tells me when she catches me looking. I can't stop staring. She looks damn cute in those black oversized frames. "They really do help."

My heart lurches in my chest. "Holy shit, you're adorable," I tell her as I lean over and press a smacking kiss on her cheek, making her laugh.

She pulls out of the parking lot, and soon we're driving through the wet London streets, Susanna peering closely over the steering wheel. She's kind of freaking me out, so I remain quiet, which enables us both to listen to Jordan and Amanda's conversation from the backseat. They're talking about me. And Susanna.

"I did mention she's the daughter of an earl?" Amanda says rather loudly. "Meaning she's nobility."

"Actually, we're distant relatives of the queen, so yes," Susanna adds. "We're technically part of the royal family." Susanna glances in the rearview mirror, and I assume she's making eye contact with Amanda. "Sorry, didn't mean to eavesdrop."

"I should apologize. We're the ones blatantly talking about you in the back of your car," Amanda says, sounding contrite.

"Saying only good things I hope." Susanna nibbles on her lower lip, looking nervous.

"I'm just giving Jordan the rundown," Amanda explains. "He didn't know who you were, so I was letting him know."

"She's my future girlfriend," I say, my voice full of pride. Damn, I couldn't stop that from coming out if I tried.

What the hell am I doing?

Susanna shoves at my shoulder, but I barely move. It'll take a lot more strength to shove me around, and she's kinda weak. "Please. You're leaving in a few days."

"I'll miss you." I mean every word, and she glances over at me, surprise filling her eyes. "You'll spend the next few days with me, right?"

"Um..."

A horn honks and Susanna jerks the steering wheel to the right, causing the Mercedes to veer sharply. Another horn sounds and she hits the brakes, glaring at me once she has everything under control.

"You're distracting me," she accuses, and I smile.

"Stop distracting her," Jordan says, his voice firm. I glance over my shoulder to see he appears thoroughly freaked out. "I want to make it to the restaurant in one piece."

"You have to leave me alone," Susanna admonishes. me "Your friend is nervous because of my driving."

"Fine." I cross my arms, clamping my hands beneath my armpits. That's the only way I can keep my hands to myself during the rest of the drive.

The minute we get in the restaurant, though, all bets are off. I'm touching her.

I'm gonna touch her all damn night.

WE'RE at a small Italian restaurant that Susanna's been to before—probably on another one of her dates—and the four of us ate so much food and drank so much wine, I know we all feel fat and lazy.

Well, I know I'm feeling that way.

But I catch Susanna ogling the dessert menu, her eyes wide and her lips parted, looking sexy as fuck, and I know she wants more.

Grabbing the laminated page from Susanna's fingers, I scan it before I suggest, "Let's order the entire dessert menu. They all sound amazing."

"That's because they *are* amazing." Susanna grabs the menu from me once more and looks it over, her lips moving as she counts the items. "But we can't eat them all, Cannon. There's too many!"

"We can try," I say with a shrug, taking back the menu again. They do all sound pretty damn good, and if we can't finish them, so what? Not like I can't afford it.

I have a little argument with the server only because he can't believe we're ordering every single dessert, and once he's gone Susanna leans toward me, her hair falling forward as she speaks.

"You indulge me too much," she murmurs, her hand resting briefly on my thigh.

"I like indulging you." I rest my hand over hers, keeping it where I want it. Too bad she's not touching my dick. "You make it easy."

She blushes prettily. "I like your friends."

I glance across the table at Jordan and Amanda, their heads bent, appearing deep in conversation.

"I'm glad. Pretty sure they like you too." I squeeze her hand and she squeezes my thigh, and all I can think about is getting her naked.

"What should we do after dessert?" She raises her brows, her expression expectant as she waits for my answer. When I take too long to speak—too captivated by her pretty face to find words—a frown appears. "You're probably tired."

"I'm not." And that's not a lie. For a man who barely got any sleep last night, I'm suddenly full of energy.

"Maybe we could go to my favorite pub. It's not too far from here," she suggests hopefully.

"You have a favorite pub?" I ask, a little surprised.

"Everyone should have a favorite pub," she scoffs, apparently offended by my question. "A place to hang out with your friends, have a few drinks and a good time. So yes, I definitely have a favorite pub."

"You are a constant surprise, do you know that?" I grab her hand and bring it to my mouth, dropping a quick kiss on her fingers. "Let's go to your favorite pub."

But I can guarantee we won't stay there for very long.

TWELVE

SUSANNA

AFTER DESSERT, we don't go to my favorite pub.

Jordan and Amanda—I adored them so much!—made their excuses and headed back to the hotel. They barely stayed for dessert. They seemed far too eager to get out of there and have some private time. I envied them in that moment. So obviously in love and able to be together with no obstacles whatsoever—how very lucky they are.

Cannon and I, there are far too many obstacles. Ones I don't want to confront tonight, so I push them aside and focus on the here and now. I'm going to take advantage of this moment and hopefully have another multi-orgasmic night like we did yesterday.

But as we exit the restaurant and make our way along the pavement, I realize I feel as if my stomach is going to explode, I'm so full of food and good wine, though I don't feel tipsy, not even a little bit.

I think all the desserts soaked up the alcohol.

"I shouldn't have sampled any of those desserts," I groan to Cannon as we find my car. One hand resting on my belly, I unlock the doors with my other hand and we both slide into the car, Cannon coming right for me before I can say or do anything.

He proceeds to maul me for approximately five minutes. We kiss and kiss until my jaw aches, and somehow during the process, Cannon turned into an octopus.

Hands everywhere. Touching me in all the right places.

Not that I'm protesting.

"Okay," I say a few minutes later when we come up for air, breathless and dizzy, shifting my dress around so it settles back into its proper place. "Shall we go to the pub now?"

He rests his hand on my knee, slowly sliding it up my thigh so his fingers slip beneath the hem of my dress. "You really want to go have a few beers, Susie?"

No. No, I do not. His fingers are crawling farther up my thigh, and when they brush against the front of my panties, all pretense of going to the pub with Cannon and drinking beer flies right out the window.

I grab my driving glasses out of the compartment I keep them in, noting how shaky my fingers suddenly are. He removes his hand from my thigh, and the disappointment that washes over me at the loss is almost overwhelming.

God, I need to get it together. Quickly.

"Back to the hotel then?" I ask, my voice extra high as I jam the key into the ignition and start the engine. I carefully maneuver the vehicle out of the parking spot and hit the gas, the car lurching forward with a squeal. "Sorry. The road's wet."

"I'm going to make something else wet too," he says, smug as can be.

"You're so rude." I shake my head and he just laughs.

"You know it's true. I can make you wet with just a look." He sends me a searing look just to prove his point and damn him, it works.

My panties grow damp the longer we stare at each other.

I realize I should be paying attention to the road and hurriedly slam my foot on the brakes before I hit the car in front of us. A long string of cars are waiting for the light to turn green and I'm sure it would've been a chain reaction collision if I hadn't braked in time.

Cannon just laughs at my bumbling ways. "You're a terrible driver," he observes good-naturedly.

"It's all your fault, with your talk of making me wet and such," I grumble, determined to keep my focus on the road and not on him.

"Making you wet and such? You act like it's no big deal." He shifts closer, his face near mine, his breath on my ear as he whispers, "I bet your panties are soaked."

Well. They are now.

"And I bet you're dying for me to touch you there."

I am. I'm dying for it.

"I bet if I reached into your panties right now, I could make you come in less than ten seconds."

A whimper escapes me and he bites my earlobe, making me jump.

"I can't wait to get you naked," he continues, his tongue darting out for a lick.

He's killing me. So is this damnable red light. We've been waiting so long it's like slow, agonizing torture.

The moment the cars start to move, I press the gas, the car lurching forward yet again, the tires squealing. Cannon settles back into his seat, still chuckling like the arrogant bastard he is. "Eager much?"

I glance over at him to see that single brow raised, a smirk curling his perfect lips. Gah, I want to kiss him, which is ridiculous considering approximately two minutes ago, we *were* kissing.

Yessss, I want to kiss him and do other things to him too. My imagination has kicked into overdrive, considering everything he just said to me.

"Maybe just a little," I admit with a smile.

"Me too." His hand drops onto my knee again, giving it a squeeze before he resumes his exploration. That hand shifts even higher, fingers teasing the inside of my thighs, and I automatically spread my legs like a wanton hussy.

Hmm, looks like I've retained some of those great words from my teenage binge of historical romance novels.

I suck in a breath when he slips those confident fingers beneath the thin fabric of my extra sexy—yes, I made sure I was wearing a better pair tonight—panties and I try my best to jerk my leg away from his explorative touch.

"If you want me to wreck the car, then keep doing what you're doing," I say, my voice nonchalant, my nerves going haywire.

I'm not exaggerating with that statement. He keeps this up and I will most likely crash my father's beloved car.

"I'll leave you alone." His hand disappears and I glance over to find him gripping both knees, his knuckles white with strain. It feels good to see he's affected by this—*thing* between us like I am. "Just know when we get back to my hotel room, you're in for it."

My entire body tingles, especially between my legs. "In for it how?"

"You want me to go into detail?"

Yes, please. "If you'd like." Again with the nonchalant tone.

He sends me a look. He sees right through me. "Honestly, I'm not sure what I want to do to you first."

"Tell me what you're considering and maybe I can help you make the decision." I can't remember where the hotel is, and I feel like a ninny for asking him. I live in London, I should know where everything is.

Do people understand just how large London is, though? And how you don't really need to ever leave your neighborhood, because all of the shops and restaurants you know and love are within a few blocks of your front door?

It's obvious I don't get out much.

"Well, I thought that lifting up your skirt the moment we get into the room, pushing aside your panties and fucking you against the door would totally work."

It would work. Yes. I agree.

"But then I thought I might prefer you lying on the edge of the bed with me kneeling between your spread legs and licking your pussy." He pauses and I glance over at him to see that deceptively innocent expression on his face. "What do you think?"

"Um..." I'm at a loss for words. I like both ideas. A lot. "You choose."

He rubs his thumb and index finger against his chin, considering both options before he says, "I think I will." And then doesn't say another word.

Torture. I swear.

"There are a few things I'd like to do to you as well," I say hesitantly, wondering if I'll have the nerve to actually say those things out loud.

"Really?" He sounds intrigued. "Like what?"

"I wouldn't mind taking off your trousers." I glance at those black trousers, stretched tight across his thick with muscle thighs. "Pulling down your boxers, and sucking your—cock until you come. In my mouth."

He says nothing, which I find so very, very interesting.

"Or maybe you could take me from behind. Both of us standing, me bent forward a little so I can take you inside me better." Ooh, yes. I've never done it standing up. It's always been a secret fantasy of mine. "And you'd grab my breasts with those extra-large hands of yours and give them a good squeeze while you fuck me repeatedly."

I'm getting into this. And he's still so strangely quiet.

"Or perhaps." I sit up straighter, my mouth stretching into a wide grin. "You could smack my butt extra hard and pull my hair while we do it doggy style." The words *doggy style* sound so silly, but the image of him doing those very things to me while I'm on all fours on that giant bed in his hotel room...

"You have a—vivid imagination," he finally chokes out, his voice strained.

I look over at him again, noting that the front of his black trousers is straining with his erection. "You bring it out in me," I tell him truthfully.

"Thank God," he mutters, making me laugh.

I come to a stop at a light—and as I look at the nearby buildings, the Caffé Nero coffeeshop to my left, I swear we've been here before. A few minutes ago, actually.

"Susie, I have a question."

"Yes?" Oh God, he knows. And he's going to give me endless shit over this.

"Are we lost?"

Slumping my shoulders, I lightly bang my head against the steering wheel once. "Perhaps."

"Why didn't you tell me?" He sounds incredulous.

"I was embarrassed. I should know my way around the city," I practically wail.

"You're ridiculous," Cannon says, but he doesn't seem mad. Instead, he grabs his phone and starts tapping. "We're ten minutes away," he says once the directions pop up on his screen. "Listen to Siri and she'll take you where you need to go."

Relief fills me as Siri directs me to turn left instead of right, which was what I've been doing. Truly I was driving in circles, and any other men I've been with in the past would've probably given me a bunch of grief about female drivers and how inferior we are. Even Colin would've said something like that. Despite his excellent sexual skills and eagerness to please, he wasn't the most progressive male I knew.

Not Cannon, though. He doesn't even seem that upset over my mistake.

If only he were a Brit. I could see myself falling in love with him so easily.

THIRTEEN

CANNON

WE FINALLY MAKE it back to the hotel, and I have to insist that Susanna get valet parking.

"It's too expensive," she protests, her lips firm.

"I'll pay for it," I tell her as one of the bellmen reaches out to open her door. She sends him a scathing look and he takes a stumbling step backward. She can play the ice queen part pretty easily when she wants to.

"No, you won't. That's such a waste of money," she says.

"I insist." I start to open the passenger side door but she reaches out to touch my arm, stopping me. I turn to look at her.

"You don't have to do this for me," she says softly. "I can find a parking spot...somewhere."

"No," I say firmly. She's being ridiculous. "I have money. Lots of it. Stop being so stubborn."

With a sigh she removes her hand and turns to look out the side window, waving the poor bellman over to her door. "Fine. Let's do this then."

We climb out of the car, and I hustle over to the bellman, explaining that Susanna is my guest, and I'd like to have valet parking, and for him to please charge it to my room. He hands me a card with a number on it, I give it to Susanna so she can stash it in her purse, and then we're entering the hotel, making our way to the elevators.

"You're so commanding," she tells me as we ride the elevator to my floor.

"What do you mean?"

"The way you just handled the valet with my car. You just took total charge of the situation." She seems impressed.

I shrug, secretly thrilled at the awe I hear in her voice. "It wasn't that big of a deal."

"It was kind of hot," she admits.

I'm smirking. I can't help it. "You find lots of things hot."

"Not with anyone else," she admits. "Just you."

Her words ring in my head as we make our way to my room, and I can't lie. They sort of freak me out.

Just you.

In a good way, though, considering I believed I was the only one who felt like this. The strong connection, the easiness between us, how much I want her, how explosive the sex is. Christ, when she told me all the ways she wanted us to do it earlier—I thought I might come in my pants, hearing her say those things in her proper accent.

Just you.

She is a complete surprise. Both fun and funny. Jordan and Amanda liked her, and that is huge in my book. I've had girlfriends before who my friends didn't like. Actually, my friends didn't like any of my serious girlfriends.

My mother used to say I always picked wrong.

Just you.

Maybe, for once, I actually picked right.

I open the door with my key card and we both practically run inside, the door closing with a loud slam behind us. I grab hold of her before she can get away from me, turning so her back is pressed against the door, my hands diving beneath her skirt so I can play with the waistband of her panties.

"Fucking me against the door wins first, huh?" she asks, sounding amused.

"You always drop the word *fuck* so easily?" I ask as I yank her panties down so they fall about mid-thigh.

"No, not usually," she says, her teeth sinking into her lower lip when my fingers sink into her pussy. "Oh my *God.*"

"You like that?" I slick my fingers through her wetness, my thumb finding her clit and pressing against it. "Damn, girl, you're so fucking wet."

"I want you," she admits, her head falling back so it hits the door softly. I increase my pace, and you can actually hear my fingers sliding through her soaked flesh. "Oh, right there. Please. *Cannon*."

My name falls from her lips again and I can tell she's already close to coming. She clamps her thighs tightly around my hand, a gasp escaping her right before she falls over the edge. Tremors race through her body, her chest heaving, her breathing loud, her pussy dripping all over my fingers as she whimpers and moans.

Those pretty little whimpers and moans have my dick trying to punch out the front of my pants, ready to break free.

"I didn't think I'd come so fast," she whispers once her breathing has somewhat evened out. Her eyes crack open and she smiles at me. "That was amazing."

"And we've only just started." I drop a kiss on her nose as I fumble with my belt buckle, trying to get it undone. Fuck foreplay and all the rest of it. I want to be inside her, fuck her hard and fast until she's gasping and coming again. I liked hearing her call my name while I gave her that orgasm.

I didn't just like it.

I fucking *loved* it.

"Let me help you," she says as she reaches for my belt buckle, batting my hands away. With a quick flick of her wrist, she has it undone, as well as the button and the zipper, and then my pants are falling to my feet and I'm kicking off my underwear while she slides her panties off. I grabbed the condom I had stashed in my front pocket and tear the wrapper open, giving my dick a firm squeeze before I roll the rubber on.

Susanna watches, her mouth hanging open, her eyes glazed with lust. She likes my dick, I know she does, and I suddenly have this fear that might be *all* she likes.

I hope to hell that's not true.

"You all right?" I ask once I have the condom fully on.

She lifts her head, her gaze meeting mine. "I'm great."

"You sure?" I touch her flushed cheek. She appears somewhat out of it. "We can wait a few minutes if you want. We can also take it to the bed if you're uncomfortable."

"You are so unbearably sweet." She wraps her hand around the back of my neck and pulls me in for a lingering kiss. One that turns into open mouths and tangled tongues in seconds. "I definitely want you to take me against this door, Cannon," she whispers into my mouth.

I break the kiss to study her, my hands going to the backs of her thighs so I can lift her up, her panties suddenly dangling from one leg. "Take you? More like fuck you," I say as I push inside her hot, tight body.

Her eyes go wide for a brief moment and she thunks her head against the door, her entire body jolting with the force of my thrusts, her eyes closing tightly. Greedily I reach for the front of her dress, clawing at the neckline, pulling it low so her breasts come into view. They're covered in white lace and satin, and I tug on her bra, pulling the cup down so I can see her rosy-pink nipple. It's hard.

So I draw it into my mouth and suck on it, making it harder.

I'm grunting like an animal with every push inside her body and she's got her hands buried in my hair, holding me to her chest. I can't stop sucking on her nipple. Laving it with my tongue. Biting it. She screams when I bite extra hard, and I speed up my pace, thrusting again and again, her ass hitting the door, her legs circled tight around my hips. We're loud, anyone who happens to pass by my room in the hall could hear us, but I just don't give a shit.

Too focused on coming, on making this woman come too. I'm overwhelmed with the primal need to mate and fuck and make her mine.

She's chanting over and over, "Don't stop, don't stop," and I won't. I can't. I feel the familiar sensation start at the base of my spine, in the pit of my stomach. I'm gonna blow. It's coming. She's tearing at my shirt, her lips finding mine, and they start going slack when she begins to orgasm. I erupt right after her, coming so hard that when it's finally over, my muscles actually ache like I just put my body through the most intense workout ever.

And I've had some intense workouts, so I know what I'm talking about.

"Wow," she whispers once she's capable of speaking again.

I'm still incapable. I swallow. Take a deep breath only to hold it, my heart thumping like a wild thing. I exhale loudly, pressing my cheek to hers and breathing in her delectable scent. She brushes my hair away from my forehead and I pull away, opening my eyes to find her watching me with seeming fascination.

"Why are we so good together?" she asks, sounding genuinely confused.

"I don't know." I drop a kiss on her lips, our bodies still fused, my dick stirring already, which is unbelievable. "It's pretty great, though."

"Definitely great," she says with a little nod. She touches my cheek. "You're sweating."

"Sorry." Most women think it's gross when a man works up a good sweat fucking them, and I'm sure the proper Lady Susanna feels the same way.

"Is it wrong to admit that I want to rub myself all over your sweaty body so I can smell like you?" She wrinkles her nose, an uncomfortable laugh escaping her. "That sounds gross, huh?"

"No." Every primal, *I am man, you are woman* need rises within me, and I'm eager to shed her clothes, shed mine, and then let her rub herself all over me. "Let's get naked and sweaty."

I pull her panties completely off and then her heels before I ease her to her feet. She sways toward me, her eyes heavy-lidded, the look of a woman who's well satisfied written all over her face. Somehow, she takes off her dress and tosses it on the floor, leaving her standing there in a bra that's half on/half off and nothing else.

She's the sexiest thing I've ever seen.

"Take your clothes off," she demands, waving a finger at me as she reaches with her other hand and undoes the clasp on her bra. It springs forward and she sheds it quickly, flinging it away so it lands on a nearby chair. I stop what I'm doing and just stare at her, taking in all the creamy, smooth skin and the big tits and the rosy nipples and the golden hair curling between her legs.

Fuck me, she is my every wet dream come true.

"Turn around first and I will," I return.

She mock pouts and I'm tempted to stuff my dick between her lips. "But then I can't see you."

"I want to see your ass," I tell her, and without a word she whips around, wagging it at me.

Kicking off my shoes and pants and underwear, I slowly walk toward her, unbuttoning my shirt, stripping it off before I stop directly in front of her. My dick is hard and waving at her ass in greeting, and I tell it to settle down.

I have other business to attend to.

Slowly I smooth my hand across one ass cheek, then the other. She is so soft. So plump. I do it again, alternating between each cheek, loving how she arches into my hand, quiet moans falling from her lips.

"You are one sexy woman," I tell her, and she glances at me from over her shoulder.

"Thank you," she murmurs, her gaze dropping to my dick. "I can't believe we're going to do this again. Already."

"Who said anything about doing it again?" I say, my eyebrows up, my fingers sneaking into her ass crack. She jumps when I touch her there and I smooth a hand over her butt once more. "Spread your legs, baby."

She does as I ask, giving me a view like no other.

"Lean forward and grab the back of the chair." How handy that it's so close.

Susanna leans forward, her tits swaying, her hands clutching the top of the leather chair. She swings her hips, her butt waving, her glistening pussy on perfect display, and I touch her there, coating my fingers with her creamy wetness, slipping two deep inside her. Her inner walls clutch me tight, like she doesn't want to let me go, and I pull out, slowly tracing the rim of her entrance.

She practically bends herself in half, resting most of her upper body on the chair in front of her, body wide open. I slide my finger from her pussy to her ass, delicately touching her ridged skin. She jumps a little but I continue my exploration, doing lazy circles, my gaze dropping to her extra wet pussy.

"You like this," I say.

"It feels so good," she practically purrs as she thrusts her butt closer. "I've—never done something like this before."

Pride surges in me that I'm showing her something new. "You're telling me I'm exploring virgin territory."

"Yes," she murmurs, jumping a little when I tease her back entry. I'm trying to get inside, but she's extra tight. "You're corrupting me."

"With pleasure," I say, making her laugh.

Does she know I mean those two words with everything I've got? She's so responsive to my touch, what I say. And she's so open. She doesn't flinch away from any of my suggestions, and she enjoys everything we do together. The multiple orgasms more than prove that.

Hell, we've barely been in my room thirty minutes and I've already made her come twice.

Deciding to give it another try, I fall to my knees and grip both butt cheeks in my hands, spreading her apart even more before my mouth lands on her pussy. Another jolt of shock runs through her at first touch, but soon she's moaning and practically grinding her pussy on my face as I continue to lick and suck. My fingers still play with her ass, and I slip my index finger inside, getting just the tip of my nail in, and a surprised "oh" sounds from her.

"Too much?" I ask after pulling away from her. My lips are soaked and I lick them, savoring her salty taste.

"No," she says with a shake of her head. "Just—be gentle."

"I plan on it," I tell her before I dive back in. I tease her swollen clit with my tongue, my finger sinking deeper and deeper, her legs growing shaky, her pussy pulsing, like she's about to come. My knees are digging into the floor, she's barely keeping herself upright, and I know we need to shift positions soon or one of us is going to collapse.

Most likely her.

I pull away from her and lay flat on the floor. "Let go of the chair," I tell her, and she glances down, frowning at me. "Sit on my face, Susie."

"Oh God," she moans as she practically collapses on top of me, her legs straddling my head, her pussy hanging right above my mouth.

"Get into a sixty-nine position," I tell her next, and she shifts. Moves. Wraps those lush lips tight around my cock as I continue to sample her pussy, and holy shit, we're both coming within minutes. What's happening between us, what we're sharing, I can't even describe it.

Actually, I can describe it in as little as three words—what we're doing is a complete fuck fest—I've never gone at it with a woman like this before, and I don't ever want it to stop.

Ever.

Sweaty and naked and covered in come, we end up wrapped around each other, still on the floor, her head nestled in that spot between my neck and shoulder, my fingers playing with her nipples as if I can't stop touching her.

And I can't.

"This is too much," she finally says, her voice low, her entire body limp as she presses it against mine.

"You tired?"

"Exhausted."

"We should get into bed," I suggest, and she shakes her head, nuzzling her nose against my neck.

"Not yet. I like how you feel wrapped around me," she whispers.

I like how she feels wrapped around me too.

Probably too much.

FOURTEEN

SUSANNA

I WAKE up to the insistent sound of my cell phone both ringing and vibrating at the same time, the most annoying sound in all the land. It stops only to start up again, and I have no idea how long this has been going on.

Or why the person calling won't leave me a bloody voice-mail and be done with it.

Reaching out, I slap my hand on top of the nightstand, trying my best to find the phone without waking Cannon. Who so happens to be sleeping behind me, the heavy weight of his cock nudged against my butt, one thick arm wrapped around my waist and holding me tight, as if he might never let me go.

The man is a giant teddy bear who I'm sure would let me snuggle up next to him all night if I wanted.

That I had the presence of mind in the middle of the night to put my phone on the charger I brought with me is impressive, considering how—*preoccupied* I was last evening. I unplug the phone and check the screen.

The name *Mother* is right there, as bold as can be.

Hurriedly slipping out of bed, I race toward the bathroom, shutting the door and answering, "Hello," in the most intelligible whisper I can manage.

"My God, how long does it take you to answer a phone these days, hmm? I thought you were dead!"

Mother can be quite dramatic, if you didn't sense that already.

"I'm fine. You should've just left a voicemail," I tell her groggily. I shuffle over to the counter, my gaze snagging on my reflection in the mirror and I almost recoil in fear.

I look...hideous. I'm naked, and I can see all my jiggly bits, every single flaw I have is on blatant display and has been since last night. My hair is curling literally everywhere, like I stuck my finger in a socket and got the greatest shock of my life. Mascara is smudged beneath my eyes, and my cheeks are puffy. I swear there are red teeth marks on my breasts and I have razor burn along the left side of my jaw.

"It's so late, Susanna. Past eleven and you're still in bed?" She sounds cross, but that's nothing new. "I thought you'd be at work."

"I work every other Monday. You know this." She does know this. She just wants to harass me for some reason.

"I want you to come to dinner," she says, changing the subject.

"All right. When?" I rub my forehead, then smooth my hair down as best I can, though I'm sure it's no help. I need a shower. And a blow out. A facial, a deep cleanse, a massage.

An all-day visit to a spa sounds like the most reasonable plan.

"Tonight."

I pause, waiting for her to say something else, but she remains quiet. "Why such late notice?"

"We need to talk. Oh, and you should bring your *friend* with you."

I'm so confused by her request. "My friend? Do you mean Evie?"

My mother hates Evie with the passion of a thousand burning suns, though I don't know why. She claims she's a bad influence, which I suppose she could be, but Evie really isn't. She doesn't push me to do naughty things. She just does them herself.

"No, of course not," she spits out, her voice laced with venom. I'm afraid her hatred for Evie will never die. "Your *other* friend. We expect you at the house at six o'clock," she chirps before she ends the call.

I stare at my phone, wondering what in the world she's talking about. My other friend? She can't be referring to Cannon, can she? How would she even know he exists, beyond my father telling her he met a nice American football player on Saturday night? Dad doesn't even know I ended up sending the night with Cannon...

Huh.

The thought hits me after I've relieved myself and I'm washing my hands. Mom does read the papers every single morning, including the overly gossipy ones that love to discuss the various socialites and young nobility out and about on the town.

Their words, not mine.

Panic filling me, I send Evie a quick text.

Have you read the papers this morning?

She tends to read them online while my mother enjoys them the old-fashioned way—delivered to her doorstep first thing every morning.

Evie's response is almost immediate.

I have. You harlot.

She adds a winky face emoji like that's supposed to make me feel better.

Why are you calling me a harlot? What did you see?

My phone rings, startling me, and I answer Evie's call.

"You don't know what's happened?" she asks incredulously.

Dread fills me, nearly sending me toppling over. "Is it bad?"

"No, you look amazing. So happy with your sparkling eyes and your hand resting on his chest." She pauses for dramatic effect, as she's wont to do. "The footballer's chest, which is as broad as a wall, I swear."

"And where did you happen to find this photo?" I ask weakly, gripping the edge of the bathroom counter. I'm suddenly dizzy.

Like I might faint.

"In the *Daily News*. It's a short piece, something about Lady Susanna Sumner catching the attention of a famous 49er visiting from the States, and what an adorable couple you two make." Evie sounds positively thrilled. "You two *are* an adorable couple. He looks at you like he wants to eat you up!"

He constantly wants to eat me up. I am so sore between my legs, I think I need a sex break. Oh, and that spa visit. "My mother just called."

Evie's good mood is deflated, just like that. "What does the Dragon Lady have to say now?" She hates my mother just as much as my mother hates her.

"She demanded that I come to dinner at the house tonight, and requested that I bring my friend."

"You know she's talking about Cannon. She must've seen the article too."

The dread rises, threatening to choke me. "If she saw the article, she must be..."

"Livid?" Evie suggests.

"No, no, not livid. More like..."

"Disappointed?"

"Yes, that's it." I don't want Cannon to meet my mother. I love her. I really do, but she's almost too...overbearing. To the point that she could scare Cannon away.

And I sort of want to keep him around as much as I can. Silly, right? What's happening between us could never work, yet I want to give it a go anyway.

Clearly, I've lost touch with reality.

"Don't let her disappointment get in the way of you living your life. You do what you want, what makes you happy. She's always trying to boss you around, and it's ridiculous, Susanna! You're a grown-ass woman. Be a boss bitch and tell her to mind her own business," Evie says.

"Have you been reading BuzzFeed articles again?" Whenever she says *grown ass woman* and *boss bitch*, I figure she's been reading up on the internet.

"They are my favorite articles to read when I'm feeling down! We all need a pick-me-up, and today, I am your pick-me-up. Cancel the dinner plans. Do your own thing. Enjoy your time with that delicious man before he hops onto a plane and flies back to California, never to be seen again. You need to savor him, my friend."

We end the call and I immediately look up the article online. Not much is said, and the photo looks like it was snapped as we left the restaurant last night. I am beaming up at him and he is looking down at me like he definitely wants to eat me up.

Yet Evie's words stay with me after our call is finished. Soon Cannon will be hopping on a plane and flying back to California, leaving me all alone for days. Weeks. Months.

Forever.

I can hardly bear the thought.

Feeling depressed, I open the bathroom door to find Cannon sitting up in bed, looking bloody magnificent with the sheets pooled around his waist, his bare chest on blatant display. He's scratching the back of his head, his golden-brown hair messy, his biceps bulging like always, his skin dark against the white bedding.

He's like my every secret fantasy come to life. He's just so... unbelievably beautiful. And kind. And sexy. And giving. And thoughtful. And amazing.

Oh, I've got it sooooo bad.

"What's going on?" he asks, his voice low and raspy, making me shiver. His hand drops from his head while I continue to stand in the doorway. "Susie? You all right?"

I think of my mother's demand, how she wants us to come to dinner tonight, and I know she'll ruin everything. I also think of the photo in the newspaper, and wonder what other papers and online sources might have said about us.

"When do you fly back home?" I ask.

He frowns. "Tomorrow afternoon."

My heart sinks. One more day. That's all I have left with him. Do I really want to waste these last hours with Cannon by going to dinner at my parents' estate and watching my mother interrogate him until he flees the house running and screaming like a maniac?

I think not.

"We have to make the most of today," I tell him as I start to approach the bed.

His gaze falls, landing on my chest, and I know he's staring at my breasts. "I'd rather stay in."

"Really?" I mock pout as I join him on the bed, scooting closer so I can climb into his lap, straddling him. The sheet is gathered between us as a sort of barrier, but I can still feel his erection beneath the fabric. "Don't you want to go out and see the sights?"

He grabs my breasts in both hands and presses them together. "This is all the sight I need to see." He bends his head and licks at my cleavage, making me giggle.

"Cannon, no. Don't you want to ride the London Eye? Go to Buckingham Palace? Check out the Tower of London? Cruise the River Thames?" I can hardly think with the way he keeps massaging and kneading my breasts. I feel like I've become his personal playground and he never wants recess to end.

"If that's what you want to do, I'm game. But if you want to stay in this room all day and mess around, I'm game for that too. Wherever you are is where I want to be." He slips his fingers beneath my chin and tilts my head up so our gazes meet. His eyes are sincere, and full of a sort of longing too. One that matches my own. "It seems like all we do is mess around, but I want you to know that I see beyond the sex stuff."

"The sex stuff?" I sort of want to laugh at what he's saying, he's so cute.

"Yeah. I see you." He drops a quick kiss on the tip of my nose. "And I like you. You're sweet and you're funny and you're...genuine. That's what I like best about you. There's nothing fake here. What I see is what I get."

"I'm a mess," I confess, suddenly embarrassed. My cheeks are hot at his thoughtful words. I suppose I don't take compliments very easily, especially not from men like him. "I look terrible after last night's...escapades."

"You look beautiful. You *are* beautiful, inside and out." This time he kisses me on the lips, a slow, lingering kiss that steals my breath and leaves me light headed. "You're right. Let's go out and see the sights for a little bit. Like that London Eye thing."

My head is swimming at all of the sweet things he just said to me, and I try to focus.

"I've never been on it," I confess.

"Really?" He sounds surprised.

"Why should I? I live here. That's a tourist trap," I explain.

"Well, today we're going to play at being tourists, you and me. Show me your city, Susanna." He cups my cheeks and kisses me, cradling my face like all dreamy boyfriends in rom-coms and romance novels do, and I practically melt into the bed at the tender gesture.

I don't know what I did to deserve his attention, but I'm going to revel in it for as long as possible.

FIFTEEN

CANNON

"THE VIEW UP HERE IS SPECTACULAR!" Susanna braces her hands on the glass like a little kid, staring at the massive city spread out before us. She glances over her shoulder to flash me a huge grin before returning her attention to the city. "You can see *everything!*"

I come up behind her, slipping my arms around her waist and resting my chin on her shoulder. "And you said you didn't want to come on the London Eye."

"I didn't say I didn't *want* to, I just...never have. Only tourists come here," she says, her lips still curved as she turns her head so her gaze meets mine. "I'm glad you wanted to go."

"I'm glad you brought me." I give her a squeeze and kiss her cheek, then release her, my own gaze snagged on the city.

We're in one of those glass capsules that spin around the Eye, giving us 360-degree views of London, and there are at least twenty other people in the capsule with us. A few of them are staring at me like they might recognize me, but I don't know.

Maybe I'm just paranoid.

Once we came up with a plan for our day, Susanna showed me the photos of us on the internet. I was floored someone cared enough to mention my name in a gossipy article. Back home, I rarely get any type of media attention, and when I do, it's usually tied to Tuttle. We played on the same high school team, so the media loved to mention that connection, especially during our first couple of seasons.

Now, though, I don't stand in the spotlight much, and I'm fine with it. I don't need a lot of attention. I just want to play ball and get paid the big bucks to do it. I'm a lucky son of a bitch and I know it.

Today, I feel even luckier than usual, and that all has to do with Susanna.

She's wandering around the capsule too, snapping endless photos on her phone. I take one of her, catching her off guard, and she shoots me a playful glare as she makes her way toward me.

"I bet I look horrible in that photo you just took," she accuses, reaching for my phone.

I hold it above my head, completely out of her reach. "Let's take one together then."

She stands just in front of me and I dip my head so our cheeks are pressed close. Holding the phone out in front of us, I snap a bunch of selfies, silently marveling at how beautiful she looks at this very moment. Her eyes are sparkling and her cheeks are pink, and her hair is the slightest bit wavy.

I'm glad I captured this moment. It's one I will remember forever.

Within minutes we're off the London Eye and then we're walking along the River Thames, dodging the many tourists with the wind brisk against our faces. I'm wearing a sweat-shirt but I'm still freezing, and Susanna is wearing a full-blown wool coat, gloves and a scarf. We stopped by her place before we started on our tourist excursion, and it was interesting to catch a glimpse of where she lives.

The flat was decently furnished, but the furniture was nondescript and the kitchen tiny—I could barely fit my monstrous ass in there. I sat on the edge of her saggy mattress and watched while she searched through her closet, trying to find the right thing to wear.

I finally grabbed hold of her waist, hauled her into my lap, told her she could go out naked for all I cared and kissed her senseless.

Funny, though, how my kissing her seemed to actually knock some sense into her head, and she was dressed and ready to go within twenty minutes.

"Where to next?" I ask as we walk side by side. I slow my pace to let her keep up with me, since my long stride equals about two to three of hers.

"Not sure. Would you like to see Buckingham Palace?"

"Is your relative the queen in the house?" I'm joking, but wouldn't it be awesome if Susanna could get me a visit with the queen?

"We're not that close of relatives. I've never even met the woman." She rolls her eyes and nudges me in the side with her elbow. "Maybe we should take a taxi. It's too far to walk, and it's already so late."

"It's only three o'clock," I point out.

"The sun sets around four or so."

Earlier than it sets at home, that's for sure.

We walk in silence, people passing by us, the street up ahead filled with traffic. A chilly wind blows off the river and I tug the hood of my sweatshirt up, trying to cover my cold cheeks.

"We should go on a hop on/hop off bus." I point at one in the near distance. "They're everywhere."

"We have to pay for them, though." She makes a little face. "And it's too expensive, considering how late it is. We won't be on it long enough to be worth the price."

We're close to the busy street, and I notice a few of those hop on/hop off buses are idling at the curb like it's a bus stop.

I also notice how most of the people are climbing on the bus and they're not showing...anything to the driver. No ticket, not a piece of paper.

Nothing.

"I have an idea," I say as I take Susanna's gloved hand.

"What do you want to do?" She starts walking faster as I practically drag her toward the buses. I don't want us to miss our chance.

"Just follow my lead," I tell her as we approach the bus.

She tries to jerk her hand out of mine. "Wait a minute. Are you doing what I think you're doing?"

I send her a look and she clamps her lips shut.

The driver isn't paying us any attention. He's too busy talking to the guy on the street who's wearing a maroon jacket with the bus company's logo emblazoned on the back. We jump on the bus and I immediately head up the narrow winding staircase to the top, Susanna right behind me.

There aren't many people sitting on the top level and we collapse into a row of plastic chairs near the back, Susanna a little breathless, me laughing my ass off.

"I can't believe you did that!" She's socking my arm with her fist, but I barely feel it.

"You did it too. You're just as guilty," I point out, still laughing.

"We're criminals!" she practically wails as the bus pulls away from the curb and heads across the bridge.

"Shh, keep your voice down. We don't want anyone else knowing we're criminals." I'm grinning again. And she's hitting me again.

And I sort of love it.

"Stop wasting your energy." I grab her wrist just as she's mid-slug. "I'd kiss your hand, but you have gloves on."

"You should kiss my lips instead." She leans in close, her mouth pursed.

I go to do just that and dodge left at the last second, kissing her cheek. She makes a disappointed noise right before I actually kiss her. I meant for it to be quick, but then I kiss her again. Then again.

Until we're full on making out on top of the tourist bus.

"We're getting carried away," Susanna says a few minutes later, after she's torn her lips from mine. Her hair is a mess from my fingers and her eyes are extra sparkly. "We don't need to make a scene."

When she gets all proper, it kind of turns me on.

"Think they'll kick us off the bus if we do?" I waggle my brows at her.

"You probably want to be kicked off, you naughty, wicked boy." She smacks my arm and then points. "Look, there's Big Ben. And the parliament building."

"Think this bus will take us to Buckingham Palace?" I ask, staring at the iconic monuments ahead of us. You see this kind of stuff in school, or online or whatever, but when it's right in front of your face, it feels almost surreal.

"Not sure. If we're lucky, it will. Seems to be going in the right direction," she answers as she looks around.

"Your sense of direction isn't the best," I tease, bumping my shoulder against hers.

She laughs. "I'm the worst. One of my faults."

"Your faults don't bother me," I murmur, slipping my arm around her shoulders so I can hold her close.

"They won't bother you because you're leaving tomorrow, and you'll never have to deal with them again," she says jokingly, but I can tell there's sadness in her words.

And those words make me sad too. They make me face reality. I'm leaving tomorrow, and Susanna's right. I won't ever see her again. There's no reason for me to.

Or is there?

SIXTEEN

SUSANNA

"THIS ISN'T REAL PIZZA." Cannon makes a mock-disgusted face as he grabs his fourth piece from the dish and bites into it, demolishing half of it in seconds.

He's complaining, yet he's eating as fast as he can breathe. Men can be so ridiculous sometimes.

"What do you mean, this isn't real pizza?" I wipe the corners of my mouth, then my fingers, before I toss my crumpled napkin on my plate. I can't eat anymore, even though I only had a piece and a half. There are too many emotions swirling deep inside of me at the moment, and I can't really control them.

Too tired. Too nervous.

Too sad.

"It's too thin. I mean, it's good, but it's not exploding with flavor like the stuff I love back home." He finishes his piece, his gaze glued to my plate the entire time. "You gonna eat that?"

"Go for it," I say, pushing my napkin away from my leftover slice of pizza.

Cannon grabs it and shoves it in his mouth, then drains the second glass of Coke the server brought him maybe five minutes ago or so. "I don't know why I'm so fuckin' hungry." He covers his mouth with a fist, hiding a burp. "Excuse me."

I study him, thoughts of my prim and proper mother flitting through my brain. She'd hate him. Despise him, really. He's ill mannered, doesn't speak proper English, definitely doesn't eat properly, and he's American.

All deadly sins in my mother's impossible-to-please rulebook.

"You okay?" he asks after a few minutes of silence. I'm sure he can sense my mood, and how quiet I've been since we entered PizzaExpress. I usually love this place. I was so excited to show it to him, to have a quiet night out to dinner before we go back to his hotel and spend the rest of the evening naked in his bed.

But my mood became more somber as the minutes ticked by. He's leaving me tomorrow afternoon.

Leaving. Me.

I don't like it. Not at all. And I know I'm being ridiculous and I barely know him, so I shouldn't be so sad. All those logical explanations sound perfectly...logical.

Yet what's happened between Cannon and me can't really be explained logically at all. And yes, we have combustible sex every single time, and I shouldn't pin our entire relationship on sexual chemistry, but I can't help it.

Our sexual chemistry is unlike anything I've shared with anyone else before. He also makes me laugh. He's sweet. He's interesting. He doesn't chastise me for my blundering ways and my bad sense of direction and the many other minor faults I know I have but can't remember.

I need to face facts. I'm a little in love with him. Not all the way, because that would surely be impossible, but a little bit?

Yes, I am. A little bit in love with Cannon Whittaker.

This giant brute of a man, a professional football player with the NFL who has scads of money and could have any woman he wants, and who happens to live in San Francisco. I will never see him again. He'll go home and forget all about me.

And I cannot stand the thought.

"I'm fine," I finally say, offering him a weak smile.

He reaches beneath the table and rests his big, warm hand on my thigh just before he leans in and whispers, "You're also a liar."

I lean my head to the side when his mouth brushes the sensitive skin below my ear, trying to fight the shiver that wants to take over. "Don't mind me. I don't want to ruin your mood."

"My mood is shit because yours is." He shifts away, his fingers slipping beneath my chin to tilt my face up, our gazes meeting. "Tell me what's wrong, baby."

I melt at him calling me baby. I also melt at the concerned glow in his eyes, the tender way he's touching me just beneath my chin. For a breathless moment I forget that we're surrounded by all sorts of people, in a crowded restaurant, spending our last night together before he leaves me forever.

But then I remember where I am. The sound of others talking, glasses clinking, music playing in the background. We're sitting at a table, right next to each other versus across, one of those obnoxious couples who can't stand it if they're not within reach of each other. The sort of couple Evie and I make fun of on a constant basis.

I've turned into *that* couple, and I don't mind one bit.

"I hate that you're leaving," I admit to him, my voice full of anguish, my throat growing tight. "Tell me I'm being ridiculous."

He brushes the hair away from my forehead, his expression sad. "You're not ridiculous. I hate that I'm leaving too, but I have to go."

"I know you have to go. You have a whole other life in San Francisco, and this—moment we're sharing is just a blip on your path." Now my chest aches, and I swear I'm minutes away from bursting into full-blown sobs.

I cannot cry in front of this man. I'll scare him to death and he'll never want to talk to me again. I can't take that risk.

"You're definitely not just a blip on my path." He grabs my hand and gives it a squeeze. "You're more than that."

I'm sure he means it, but tonight, with his departure only hours away, his words are...

Meaningless.

We remain quiet for a while, the world going on around us, until the server stops by to check on us and Cannon requests the bill.

"Do you need some money?" I ask once the server is gone, reaching for my bag.

He grabs my arm and stops me. "Absolutely not. This is my treat."

I let him pay. He's paid for everything since we've met. Mother can't criticize him for not being a gentleman, because he so is.

Not that she'll ever meet him, so...I guess I never have to worry about her criticizing him either.

The moment the bill is paid, Cannon is leading me out of the restaurant and into an Uber he ordered. The drive is short since the hotel is thankfully close, and we're locked away in his room in minutes, both of us still quiet and, oddly enough, not immediately reaching for each other either.

I feel suddenly shy. Perhaps he's aware of my change of mood and doesn't know how to approach me either. He's clear on the other side of the room, standing at the window that overlooks the city while I'm hovering near the door, wringing my hands and wondering what I should do next.

"Do you want to go home?"

Cannon's deep voice knocks me from my thoughts, startling me.

"Do you want me to go home?" I ask in return.

An irritated sound escapes him and he runs a hand through his hair before turning to face me. "You're hanging out by the door like you're gonna make a run for it, so I thought you might want to bail."

"I..." I straighten my spine, my gaze meeting his. I need to be truthful. "I don't want to bail."

"Well, come here then." He waves a hand, his expression weary, and I go to him, gasping when he hauls me into his arms and squeezes me tight. "We can't act like this, Susie. These are our last hours together before I leave. We have to make them count," he murmurs close to my ear.

I close my eyes, fending off the tears that threaten to spill. I know he's right. We need to shift the mood and soon, or else we'll end up having sex and crying in each other's arms for the rest of the evening.

The having sex part sounds wonderful, but the crying part sounds bloody awful.

And just like that, an idea comes over me.

"You need to say something," I murmur into the solid wall of his chest.

"What was that?" He wraps his hands around my shoulders and pulls away from me, putting some space between us.

"You need to say something," I repeat, hoping he'll know what I'm referring to.

Judging by the tremendous frown on his handsome face, he's not understanding what I'm trying to say. "Like what?"

"Something—dirty." My cheeks go hot. "To change the mood."

Realization lights his eyes and he nods, a sexy smirk appearing on his face. "You want me to start up the dirty talk?"

I nod hurriedly, my head bobbing like I'm an out-of-control doll. "I think it might help."

"I'm sure you do." He chuckles, and the tension between us has already shifted. "Whatcha you want me to say?"

"Isn't that your area of expertise? Figuring out what to say?"

"Hmm." He rubs his chin, I can hear his fingers rasping against the stubble growing there, and I want to rub against him. Feel the sharp prick of his newly forming beard scrape against my sensitive skin. "I know you like it when I talk about making your pussy wet."

"You're right." A tingle starts low in my belly, and I nod my encouragement. "Do go on."

Another chuckle escapes him and he studies me with a peculiar gleam in his eye. "Want me to lick that sweet pussy of yours, or stroke it first?"

My knees grow wobbly. "Whatever you prefer," I tell him after I clear my throat.

"Uh huh." He crooks his finger and makes the universal "come here" signal. "Get your pretty ass over here, Lady Susanna."

I do as he says, practically sprinting so I can reach him in as few steps as possible. He hooks his arm around my waist and hauls me in, his mouth landing on mine in a searing kiss. All I can think is *yes, yes, YES* as his tongue tangles with mine, as his big hand grips my hip and his other hand grips my right breast. He is all brute strength and unrefined kissing and groping, and it is absolutely marvelous.

He breaks the kiss first, breathing hard, his eyes blazing with passion as he studies me. Again, I sound like a historical romance from my teenaged past, but I don't really care. In fact, I loved those romance novels and believe I should go in search of them at my parents' house the next time I visit.

"You taste good," he says just before he kisses me again. "I can't get enough," he murmurs against my parted lips.

My entire body goes weak at his words. Colin was all action but very little talk. We were young and I didn't expect it. Would've probably burst out laughing if he'd tried, uncomfortable and embarrassed.

Cannon is all talk *and* action. A double whammy of the good stuff. He not only makes delicious sexual promises, he keeps them. He's kissing me again, and his hands are everywhere at once, fingers seeking and sliding beneath the waistband of my leggings. His fingers slide in between my legs, discovering the lacy pair of panties I'm wearing, and he pulls away a little so our gazes can meet.

"I like your underwear."

"You haven't even seen them." My breath hitches when his exploring fingers dive beneath the thin fabric of my panties.

"I don't need to see them to know I like 'em. I definitely like the way they feel." His mouth is on mine once more, and I'm drowning. In his taste, in his panting breaths and growling sounds and assured touch. In his hands and his body and his words and those low, rumbling groans he makes in the back of his throat.

He somehow walks me backward and the next thing I know, I'm falling. Falling onto the bed, Cannon following me, his body pinning me into the mattress. He's removing my clothing, dropping a kiss wherever his hands touch me and I almost want to cry, it feels so good.

Yet I don't cry. I keep it together, reminding myself now is not the time for tears. My eyes pop open and I watch as he removes my jumper, then my leggings, until I'm lying there in a pair of pink lacy panties and a matching bra that does little to contain the spillage of my overabundant breasts.

"Damn, woman," he says, whistling low as his appreciative gaze rakes over me. "I could stare at you like this all night."

That is the very last thing I want him to do. I might combust with wanting him.

"Please don't do that," I say, whimpering when he draws the back of his hand across my quivering stomach.

"Don't do what?" he asks with a frown, his gaze zeroed in on my chest.

"Stare at me all night," I explain, my voice shaky.

He reaches for the spot between my breasts, fingers drifting across the satiny band of my bra before they slide up into my cleavage. "You'd rather I touch you all night?"

His fingers dive beneath the lacy bra cup, tweaking my already hard nipple and making me gasp. "Please," I choke out.

"I'm a multitasker. I can stare and touch at the same time," he says with a grin just before he dips his head and ravages my exposed breasts with his mouth. He kisses and licks the sensitive skin, making me yelp and jump in surprise, just before I moan and dissolve into the mattress.

He reaches behind me and unsnaps my bra, tugging it off with impatience. I just lie there on the bed, letting him have his way with me, moaning when he pulls my nipple into his mouth and sucks until I feel borderline delirious. My hands land in the softness that is his hair and I tunnel my fingers through the thick strands, tugging and pulling and moaning and basically acting the fool.

I don't think Cannon minds, though. Actually, I'm fairly certain he's into it.

Into me.

How did I get so lucky?

SEVENTEEN

CANNON

I CREEP around the hotel room quietly, trying to pack my stuff without disturbing the sleeping princess in my bed. She's naked save for the sheet twisted around her lower half, hair strewn across the pillow and her arms thrown above her head, the glorious perfection that are her tits on blatant display.

Distraction is not the name of the game this morning. Actually, it's almost the afternoon, and I need to head to the airport in less than an hour.

But I don't want to.

I already cleaned out the bathroom, shoving my toiletry bag in my suitcase. A soft little moan comes from the bed and I perk up, on high alert for another one of those sounds.

I'm gonna miss those sounds.

Her.

I'm gonna miss her real bad.

Giving up all pretense of packing, I climb into bed and snuggle up behind her, my cock making a tent of the towel that's still somehow wrapped around my waist. I push it away and toss it on the floor, positioning Susanna so I can nestle my erection in the crack of her plump ass.

She stirs, rubbing her butt against my cock, and I swear my eyes cross. I grab hold of her hips to keep her still, thankful the box of condoms is on the bedside table closest to me. I might need to reach for one on a moment's notice.

"I thought you were getting ready to leave me," she murmurs.

Bending down, I drop a kiss on her neck. "I thought you were sleeping."

"Hmm, I was pretending. Hoping I might wake up and find this was all just a dream."

I'm a little disturbed by what she said. "That me and you were a dream?"

"No, that you having to leave is a dream." She tilts her head so she can look up at me. "Can't you just give up your life and stay here with me?"

I know she's kidding, but I'm half tempted.

Damn it, I really like this woman. A lot. Probably too much. I could say it's just sex, but I'd be lying. There's no denying the sex is good, yet there's more between us.

For the first time in my life, I feel like there's so much more.

And I can't do anything about it.

I reach around so I can cover her breasts with my palms, kneading them gently. She practically purrs as she rubs her butt against me once more, her arms rising so she can clasp the back of my neck and thrust her boobs into my hands. She kicks the sheet away so her nakedness is completely on display, and I pause, studying her.

She's beautiful. All lush, creamy skin and pink nipples and an even pinker pussy that tastes so damn good I can see myself getting a craving.

Screw that, I already have a craving.

I pluck at her nipples, tugging and pulling, noting how her legs scissor against mine, her body getting restless for me. Because she wants me.

Just as much as I want her.

"One last time?" I ask her, my hand drifting across her belly to settle on that needy spot between her thighs.

"Please." Susanna spreads her legs a little, letting my fingers slip inside. She's hot and wet, and with my other hand I reach for the open box of condoms, thankful when I get one between my fingers.

Releasing my hold on her, I open the condom wrapper and slip the rubber on, giving my cock a good tug after I roll the condom in place. I grasp her hips once more and slide in with ease, she's so wet and used to me after all the fucking we did last night.

A moan escapes her and I close my eyes, breathing in her scent as I press my face into her hair. I keep still, my cock giving a little twitch every few seconds, urging me to get on with the show, but I don't want to. Not yet.

I'm trying to draw this out as much as I can.

But Susanna's impatient, and eventually, so am I. I give in to my needy dick and start pounding into her, my hands grasping as much of her ass I can, our bodies slapping against each other with my every thrust. Until we're both groaning and coming and I shudder and shake, our mutual orgasms leaving us both gasping for air once it's over.

The euphoric high from coming crashes in an instant when I realize that this is the last time I'll fuck Susanna for a while.

Maybe even the last time *ever*.

"I need to get ready," I tell her, pulling out of her body and heading for the bathroom so I can dispose of the condom. I keep my distance as I toss on a T-shirt and my underwear, then pull on a pair of black joggers. I gather up the rest of my clothes piled on the floor and dump them into the suitcase that's sitting open on one of the hotel chairs.

Susanna is getting ready too. Pulling on a dark gray sweater and pair of leggings that she packed in the bag she brought with her yesterday, not even bothering with putting on a bra or a pair of panties, which surprises me. She tugs her hair back into a ponytail, her expression so forlorn that just looking at her breaks my heart.

So I keep busy and keep my focus off of her, checking my phone real quick to make sure I have my boarding pass in the airline app and that the flight hasn't been delayed or canceled.

Unfortunately, it's right on time.

But her mood permeates the room, and my mood is just as bad. It's hard enough, having to leave her like this. Seeing her so sad, knowing that I'm the cause of her sadness, is not easy to deal with.

I'm zipping closed my suitcase when I feel her come up behind me. When she wraps her arms around my waist and clings to me, her cheek pressed against my back, I heave a deep sigh, resting my hands on top of hers.

"You'll let me know you make it home safely?" she asks, her voice quiet.

"Definitely." I curl my fingers around hers and give them a squeeze. "We'll keep in touch, Susanna."

"Of course we will," she says faintly, and I know she doesn't believe me.

I turn to face her, cupping her cheeks in my hands, my gaze locking with hers. "I mean it. These last few days have been amazing. I promise I will never forget you."

She laughs, but there's no humor there, and her eyes seem to glaze over with tears, though they never fall. "You talk like that and it sounds like you already have forgotten me."

I say nothing. There's nothing more to say. Maybe she's right. And maybe it's best if I do forget her. Let her go on with her life so I can also go on with mine.

Instead of saying all that, I dip my head and kiss her gently, my lips clinging to hers. "Don't forget me," I whisper when we finally break apart.

Another laugh escapes her, this one watery and full of emotion. "I could never."

"Want to go with me to the airport?" I ask hopefully.

"Not a chance." She says the words so quickly, I step away from her, startled. "I'm sorry, but I can't stand the thought of waving goodbye to you at the airport and having to leave the place alone and...empty."

"I can't stand the thought of leaving you in this hotel room all alone," I tell her, wishing she knew just how hard this entire situation is for me.

"Then let me make it easier on you." Now it's her turn to gather up her stuff, and she throws it all in that small duffel bag she brought, not bothering to make sure if any of her clothes are folded.

Funny, how being around her for only a few days, I already know that's nothing like Susanna usually behaves.

"I'm going to leave first," she tells me once she's packed all of her belongings. Her smile is sunny bright, her eyes a little wild, her usually sleek hair curling around her face despite the ponytail. "Goodbye, Cannon. I'm so glad I got to meet you."

I haul her into my arms before she does something crazy like offer her hand for me to shake. She's clinging to me again, her face pressed against my chest, and I rest my chin on top of her head, simply holding her for as long as I can.

Eventually, she pulls away, grabs hold of her duffel bag and purse, then makes her way to the door.

I'm frozen in place, watching her go, watching her walk right out of my life, and there's this bossy ass voice in my head that sounds just like my high school football coach. It won't stop yelling at me, saying things like,

Stop her!

Don't let her go!

You're just going to let her leave?

Chase after her!

Tell her to come to California with you!

I don't say anything like that, and I don't try and stop her either. For once in my life, I'm trying to make a mature decision. Convincing this beautiful woman that she belongs to me is not the right choice. We both should move on.

We don't really have any other choice but to move on.

She rests her hand on the door handle and hesitates, her back to me, and like an idiot, hope rises in my chest, making my heart thump extra hard.

What's she gonna do?

What's she gonna say?

I wait in anticipation for her to speak.

She doesn't. Glancing over her shoulder, she offers me a weak smile and a whispered goodbye, then opens the door and slips through it. It slams behind her with such force, I almost jump out of my skin.

Just like that, she's gone.

I speed up my packing process, thankful I got a car arranged for me last night and it'll be here in a few minutes. Once I have everything shoved into my suitcase, I'm out the door as well, riding down the elevator and letting the recent memories run through my brain like the most painful montage ever created.

I've had the best time of my life over the last few days, all because of a woman. A woman I'm leaving behind.

The elevator doors slide open less than a minute later, shoving me into reality. People mill about the lobby, there's music playing and I hear horns honking on the street just outside the door. Wincing against the sudden noise and light, I stride through the cavernous lobby, keeping my head down so I won't make eye contact with anyone, when I hear a familiar sweet voice call my name from behind me.

Whirling around, I see Susanna coming for me at full speed, her expression full of pure determination. I forget about my suitcase, abandoning it so I can run toward her, meeting her halfway. I pull Susanna into my arms and swing her around and around with my face buried in her hair, breathing her in one last time.

"I couldn't leave you without giving you a proper goodbye," she whispers.

I pull away so I can study her pretty face, see the tears filling her eyes, streaking down her cheeks, and my heart cracks wide open. "We can make this work."

She blinks up at me, frowning. "What do you mean?"

"You and me. Me and you. Us. We can be together. Long distance," I explain, not sure where this is coming from.

All thoughts of doing the right thing flew right out the window, I guess.

"It would be *very* long distance between us. You do realize this, don't you?" Her brows pinch together and she's frowning, yet she's still the cutest thing I've ever seen.

I can't help but laugh. "I know, baby. But I think we can make it."

She says nothing for a moment, still blinking up at me with the tears streaming down her cheeks, and I wipe them away with my thumbs. "I think you're completely mad."

Mad? Oh. Right. She means crazy. "But that's your favorite quality about me, am I right?" I grin and she rises up on tiptoe to kiss me on the mouth. I cup the back of head, keeping her there, and when I finally break the kiss, I murmur against her lips, "Tell me you want to give this a shot. That you want to be with me."

"I don't know..." Her voice drifts and I kiss her again. Hard and fast.

"Just say yes," I practically demand.

She's smiling through the tears, nodding continuously. "All right. Yes. *Yes.* We can make this work."

"You're right." I kiss her again before she reconsiders what she just said. "We can definitely make this work."

EIGHTEEN

SUSANNA

"THIS IS NEVER GOING TO WORK."

I hang my head at Evie's words, disappointment leaving me weary. That's the last thing I want to hear from my best friend. The moment I walked into my tiny flat, I was overwhelmed with such sadness I called Evie and begged her to meet me for dinner. She grumbled and complained and finally agreed, and now here we are, at one of our favorite restaurants in my neighborhood. We were seated quickly, the waiter giving us menus and taking our drink orders, and when he walked away, I launched into a quick rundown of my last few days spent with Cannon.

Well, almost everything. Some things are better left unsaid, you know? They're private. Sacred to me.

Yes, I will really keep to all that private, sacred talk this time around. There's no need for me to spill every single detail about my time with Cannon.

"You don't think it will?" I finally ask her, my gaze locked on the menu, even though I already know what I'm going to order.

"Susanna, be realistic. He lives in San Francisco, you live here. He's a celebrity, you're the daughter of an earl, but you're not a *celebrity*. Well. Perhaps you are, but not like he is. Right? Or am I wrong…" Her voice drifts and I lift my head to find her watching me.

"I'm definitely not a celebrity. I'm no Meghan Markle," I practically sputter, making Evie laugh.

"Right. Okay. Well, he makes millions, and most likely gets endorsements for posing in his underwear or something along those lines. And there are probably loads of beautiful women throwing their panties at him on a daily basis. Without you around, he will slip up." At my look of horror, she sighs. "He's a *man,* darling. That's what they do," Evie explains, smiling up at the server when he brings her the dirty martini she requested earlier. "Thank you, you're a doll."

He smiles in return, puffing up his chest.

I say nothing, just glower at both of them until he finally flees.

"He's not a cheater," I say, watching as she gulps down the dirty martini like she's been wandering the desert for the last month and finally came upon an oasis. "He told me he's over that whole football groupie scene."

Evie practically snorts into her drink, then sets it on the table. "Of course he'll tell you that. He's saying whatever you need to hear, as long as he can dive into your knickers."

She doubts all men after having a few bad experiences. Okay, some of them were really bad, *awful* experiences, but she doesn't have the best taste, and she knows it.

It's the wildness in her—all that spontaneity is bound to get you in trouble sometimes, right?

"He's not a liar either," I say in his defense, but she doesn't answer me. Just shoots me a look that I'm full of crap. "And besides, I was ready to let him go."

I was. Really. I walked out of that hotel room with my head held high and my tongue firmly between my teeth. I wasn't going to beg and plead, and I wasn't about to make any outrageous suggestions.

I cried in the elevator. And I cried in the lobby. Then I waited, fully planning on torturing myself while I watched him leave the hotel without any knowledge that I was lurking there like some sort of deranged stalker.

But when I saw him, my chest grew tight. My heart raced. I even became dizzy. The misery was etched all over his face, leaving him looking raw and vulnerable, and I went into pure survival mode.

I chased after him like a loon and somehow it turned into us committing to each other. He asked me to be his girlfriend, and I agreed.

Still can't quite believe I did that, either.

"Ready to let him go, my arse." Evie snorts again, and I wonder when she developed this unappealing habit. "You planned that entire fiasco."

"It wasn't a fiasco, and I didn't plan it." I love Evie, but sometimes she's *too* honest. "Humor me for a bit. Tell me I did the right thing."

"Yes. You did the right thing." She waves a hand, rolls her eyes. Takes another slurp from her martini glass. "It's not going to end well, Susanna. You two will have this farce of a long-distance relationship, you'll go over to California at least once and he'll show you Disneyland and Alcatraz and all that shit, and maybe he'll come back over here and meet the family, which will end him right there, but we won't focus on that right now. Anyway, you'll pretend that you're in a relationship and tell everyone your boyfriend is that hot footballer from California, and then some gossip site will have a photo of him with some trashy bleached blonde American girl hanging all over him. She's nineteen and the coach's daughter and they'll get married. The end."

I blink at her, startled by her words, hating how they swirl around in my brain like she just spoke the truth.

She plucks the toothpicked-olive out of her drink and waves it at me before popping it in her mouth. "You know that's how it'll happen," she says as she chomps on the olive.

A shudder moves through me. Both at the rude way she's speaking to me and the fact that she's talking with her mouth full. "It will not."

"Fine, it won't. You two will suffer miserably through your long-distance relationship and eventually come out on the other side. He'll ask you to marry him, you'll say yes, and your mother will convince your father to cut you from the family inheritance. Thank God the footballer is rich or else you'd really be in a pickle."

"Evie," I scold, leaning across the table so I can hiss at her and not scream like I really want to. "Why are you being so dreadfully negative?"

"I don't want to see you get hurt," she says, mimicking me so that she's leaning across the table too. "This won't end well. You're just too—lovesick to see it."

"You think I'm in love with him?" It's like I want to hear her say that very thing.

"I don't know. Are you?" Her brows shoot up.

The server chooses that exact time to arrive at our table, and we give him our order, me deciding on water versus any sort of alcohol to drink. I need to get some actual sleep tonight, and drowning my happy/sadness in liquor isn't the answer.

"I'm not sure," I tell her once the waiter is gone.

Evie smirks, then polishes off the rest of her martini in one swallow. Lucky for her she ordered another one from our newly besotted waiter. "You're just under his sex spell. Give it some time and distance, and you'll eventually come to your senses."

Hmm. She could be right. He did cast a sex spell over me, one that I was fully committed to. I still cannot believe some of the things we did together. I've never been so daring or adventurous in bed. Ever.

Not even with Colin.

"He's better than Colin," I admit. "I know that."

"Let's be real, Susanna. Everyone you dated after him was better than Colin. He was an overly enthusiastic eighteen-year-old boy who gave you your first orgasms, so of course you thought he was the most amazing thing to ever happen to you." Evie shakes her head. "Did you ever talk to this man? Like have real conversations?"

"Actually, we talked quite a bit. About all sorts of things." When we weren't desperate for each other, we did have great conversations. I'm not only attracted to Cannon, I really like him as a person, and that says a lot.

Most of the men from my not-so-distant dating past, I didn't know what to think about. We usually had nothing in common, or zero chemistry, or they were dreadfully boring. Or pompous asses. Anyone my mother tried to set me up with, well...it always ended up a complete failure.

She has different expectations from me than I have from myself, that much is clear.

"Do you think your parents will like him?" Evie asks.

"My father met him." For all of about a minute. "He seemed quite taken with him." Quite taken with his enormous size.

Evie makes that *hmm* face she often does when she has to concede that what I'm telling her isn't a load of rubbish. Though I kind of am spewing a bunch of lies. Not that I'll ever admit it. "That's a positive sign. Maybe he could convince your mother that Cannon Whittaker is a good match for you."

I wouldn't go that far. "Perhaps. Though they really didn't talk as much as I would've liked."

"Oh well. That's concerning then." Evie reaches across the table and rests her hand on top of mine. "I'm happy for you, I really am. And if I'm being too negative, it's only because I'm trying to watch out for you. I don't want this man to hurt you."

"I know," I murmur, hanging my head once more. "You have my best interests at heart."

"It's true. I do. And that's why I worry about your mother as well. She doesn't like any of the men you've ever dated, save for the few she's tried to set you up with, and those never worked out," Evie explains.

"She'd hate Cannon," I blurt, unable to hold back any longer. "I know she would. He's rather crass, and the way he speaks sometimes isn't very proper, and he eats with his mouth open."

Evie's expression is pure sympathy, so I continue, "But not all the time, only when he's particularly hungry." Which seems to be all the time, not that I'll mention it. "He can be rather loud, and he's just so...*large.* She'll hate him for his size alone, I know she will."

"That's a terrible reason to hate someone," Evie says, her voice low, her eyes narrowed. She loves talking badly about my mother. "Just because he's large."

"That's my mother for you, though. She won't approve. He doesn't have a title, he doesn't come from a noble family, and he's American. All negatives in her rule book."

Evie scowls. "Your mother is horrible."

And that's my cue to change the subject, which I do with ease. I ask Evie about her love life and usually that's her cue to regale me with all sorts of sordid tales.

But she remains mum, surprisingly evasive, which makes no sense whatsoever. When the server eventually arrives with our meals and Evie's second dirty martini, she flirts with him shamelessly. Even batting her eyelashes at him and flashing him a bit of leg, which is completely over the top.

Just watching her makes me miss Cannon. Why, I'm not sure. Maybe because I don't have to try very hard and he's instantly interested in me?

"The waiter is cute," Evie says once he leaves. "Think I should give him my number?"

"Give him your Snapchat. It's safer. Then he can't call and terrorize you," I say, pushing my fork around my plate. Guess I'm not as hungry as I thought I was.

"Maybe I want him to terrorize me." She grins, her eyes sparkling, and I blame the martinis. "You've had a good terrorizing the last couple of days. Now it's my turn."

"Cannon didn't terrorize me," I say, a little irritated at her choice of words.

"Hmm, well he certainly did *something* to you, considering how you're all glowy and in love after a mere three days," she mutters.

"Four," I correct. "We spent four days together."

And that's insane, right? I see what Evie is trying to say. Four days with a man and I'm willing to maintain a long-distance relationship with him. If this were Evie, I'd try my best to convince her this was a terrible idea.

Because it is. A terrible idea. I must remember that. Remember, too, her wise words about how a little time and distance will change everything. It will.

I'm sure of it.

NINETEEN

CANNON

"I MISS YOU." I'm lying in bed on a Friday night, and it's only five-thirty. But I'm under the covers and naked, Face-Timing with Susanna, contemplating whipping out my dick so she can get a good look at what she's missing.

It's one-thirty in the morning where she's at, and she's actually in bed for real, her eyes puffy, her hair a mess, and I think she's naked.

"I miss you too," she says, sounding groggy. "I set an alarm so I'd wake up before you called."

"You were sleeping?" I'd be pissed, having to wake up from a sound sleep just to talk to someone like me.

Maybe this is a sign that she actually cares?

"I wanted to actually see your face. This time difference is a killer." She yawns, the sheet falling down a little bit, revealing the tops of her breasts.

My cock stirs, reminding me that it wants to make an appearance eventually.

"You gonna show me your tits?" I ask, scrubbing a hand over my face.

Her eyes go wide. "You say the crudest things." The sheet falls completely and then there's a bunch of rustling, the camera shifting away from her so I'm looking at her tiny bedside table. "Hold on," she calls.

And then her breasts fill my phone screen for a few seconds, giving me the perfect view. "What do you think?" she asks, her voice sounding distant, like she's far away.

"I wish I could suck on them," I say wistfully.

"Oh, Cannon." She jerks the camera back to her face and she's shaking her head, though she looks pleased. "You can't just—say things like that."

"Why not? I'm telling the truth. And that's what you want to hear, right? Not a bunch of crappy lies."

"I absolutely want to hear the truth," she says, her voice soft. I stare at her pretty face, momentarily entranced. "How was practice today?"

We've been texting constantly since I arrived back in California, chatting whenever we can, and finally I had to plan a FaceTime date just so I can see her damn face. After spending so much time with Susanna, not having her around feels...weird. Like I'm missing a limb or something. And I'm not embarrassed to tell her I miss her either.

Thank God she said she missed me too. I don't want this to be a one-sided relationship thing.

We need to be in this together.

"Practice was brutal. The coaches ran us hard, though I'm starting to think it was a normal practice and we're all still extra tired after coming back from the UK," I tell her.

We've been back for about a week. If my words sound like a fucking excuse, that's because they are.

"Aww, poor baby." She's teasing, I can tell by the sound of her voice, the smile on her face. "If I were there, I bet I could make it better."

"You give me a view of your naked body and I'll definitely be feeling better," I tell her immediately.

A nervous laugh escapes her. "I can't do that."

"Why not?"

"It's..."

"What couples do when they're apart." I sit up more and the blanket drops so my chest is exposed. "Show me what you got, beautiful."

She presses her lips together, contemplating my suggestion before she scoots back a little and lets the sheet drop once more, her bare chest coming back into view, though now I can also see her pretty face. "There you go."

I nod. "Yeah. Right there. Nice."

Her cheeks go pink. "You're wicked."

"You like it."

"I do," she says without hesitation.

"Let's get naked," I suggest.

Worry crosses her face. "Do you think we should?"

Now it's my turn to answer without hesitation. "Fuck yes."

More laughter, the cheerful sound making me miss her so damn much, I'm almost overwhelmed. This is crazy. "You get naked first," she says.

I whip the sheet back and scan my phone camera over my body, lingering on my rising dick. "Your turn."

"Goodness, you're huge."

"Every inch is for you, baby. Now show me what you got," I say.

"You're really going to make me do this, aren't you?" She looks around, then sets her phone against something, the camera still angled directly at her bed. She tugs back the covers, revealing that she's lying there in a pair of black panties and nothing else, and when she kicks them off, I suck in a sharp breath at seeing her naked.

"I feel ridiculous," she tells me as she lies on her side on the mattress, head propped on a pillow, her legs crossed so I can't see that delectable spot between her thighs.

"You look pretty fucking amazing." I wrap my hand around the base of my cock, giving it a stroke. "I could get off just looking at you."

Her eyes go wide and she chews on her lower lip. "Are you going to—*masturbate?*"

I burst out laughing. "I thought that was the plan."

"I've never done this sort of thing before," she admits, sounding prim.

Damn, I love it when she talks like that. Sounds like that. Little Miss Proper makes me wanna go wild on her.

"Jerked off on camera?"

"I don't jerk off, Cannon," she says, sounding irritated, but not really. I think she's just giving me a hard time. "But yes, if you're referring to masturbating with each other while on FaceTime, that's a definite first for me."

I love that I can be some of her firsts. "How about sexting? Ever done that?"

She makes a little face. "Not really."

"You've never sent a guy a sexy text before?"

"Define sexy text," she says.

I gather up some of my pillows and push them to the side so I can prop my phone against them, then get comfortable, hopefully most of my body in view as I continue talking to her. "Something like, can't wait to taste your cock in my mouth?"

She blinks a little. "That's rather..."

"Sexy?" I wrap my fingers around my cock, and I see that she's watching me.

Good.

"Yes. Um, definitely."

"You should say it then," I suggest, my voice casual.

"That I can't wait to taste your cock in my mouth?" she asks.

"Yeah, just like that." I start to stroke my erection, slowly, sort of playing with it, and I see she's not doing a damn thing. "You gonna touch yourself?"

"Should I?"

"Absolutely," I say with an encouraging nod.

"This is just so...weird." She's giggling as she wiggles around, trying to get more comfortable, I assume. Then she's lying directly in front of the camera, her head and upper body propped on her pillows, her legs spread wide so all I can see is her face, her breasts, her belly and her pussy.

All of her pussy, every pretty pink part of it.

"Damn, woman," I mutter, increasing my pace for only a few seconds before I slow back down. I don't wanna blow yet. "You're showing me *everything*."

"You don't want to see it?" She starts to close her legs and I yell, making her pause. "I guess you do," she says as she slowly widens her legs once again.

"Touch yourself," I whisper, and I watch as her fingers hover above her pubic hair for a brief moment before they slide down, down, until she's tentatively touching herself, just like I asked her to.

"Feels good?" I ask, my gaze glued to her busy hand.

"Sort of. I wish you were the one touching me," she admits, her fingers still moving, her breaths coming faster.

"Pretend it's me, baby. Touching that pretty pussy and making it good and wet." She increases her pace at my words and I swear I can hear her fingers moving through her juicy folds. That only turns me on more. "So beautiful."

"You like watching?" Her voice catches when she must touch a particularly sensitive spot and a little whimper escapes her. "I like watching you."

"Yeah?" I stroke my cock harder. Faster. "I wish you were touching me."

"I wish I was touching you too." Her fingers work furiously on her pussy.

"I want your mouth on my cock, so I can come down your throat." I'm panting. I'm also sweating. It didn't take long for us to get out of control.

"I'd drink down every last drop too," she tells me.

Shit. I close my eyes, imagining me coming all over her parted lips. The familiar feeling is there, bearing down on me, and I try to withstand it a little bit longer. "I bet you would, greedy girl."

Her eyes flare and she lifts her hand, her fingers glistening. "I'm feeling extra greedy tonight," she tells me.

Just before she slips her fingers into her mouth and sucks on them.

Loudly.

That's it. I come all over my hand, a shuddery groan leaving me as my stomach heaves. I've been a walking hard-on since I left London over a week ago, tense and on fire for only one woman.

Susanna.

I hear a moan and realize it's her. My eyes pop open just in time to watch as she comes, her fingers working their magic between her clenched thighs, her head thrown back and her eyes closed, a keening sound falling from her lips. I watch in fascination, a residual shiver taking over me, and when it's all over and she's lying there like a limp doll, I finally have to say something.

"You are so fucking hot," I breathe.

She opens her eyes and starts to laugh. And I laugh too. Both of us laugh together for a few minutes, spent and exhausted and exhilarated and feeling so damn alive.

I'm overwhelmed too. Emotional. I'm ready to spill my guts, let her know how I truly feel about her, about us, but at the last second, I clamp my lips together, triumphantly fighting off the urge to confess all.

She'd only think I was saying all that because I just came. And maybe that's the case.

I'm not sure.

"I wish you could come out to California soon," I say, my voice wistful.

Damn, I sound like a needy bastard. Maybe because I am one.

"I wish I could too, but there is no way that's happening until you meet my parents," she says, her prim and proper tone back despite her lying there naked as the day she was born.

"I thought you were an independent single woman." I'm teasing, but there's some truth to my words. Does she really have to get her parents' permission to travel out of the country? She's twenty-three years old, for Christ's sake. She's younger than me but still a full-blown woman.

"I am, but a trip like that...is momentous. My father doesn't like the idea of me being an independent single woman. He wouldn't want me traveling alone," she says.

"I already met your dad, remember?"

"Of course I remember, but you two met in a more casual sense, you know?" She wrinkles her nose. "If we're really in a—*relationship*, then they'll want to meet you under more formal circumstances."

"Like how?" I'm truly baffled. My dad isn't even in my life, hasn't been for years, and though I want my mom to like the woman I'm in a relationship with, it wouldn't make or break that relationship if she didn't.

As in, it's *my* relationship. The only opinions that matter are mine and my girl's.

"They'll want you to come to the house, and have dinner with us. Spend time together as a family," she explains. "You'll need to meet my older brother as well."

I forgot she had a brother. She doesn't mention him too much. "Your brother is a cool dude?"

"I wouldn't call George—cool." She smiles. "He's rather stiff, like my mother."

I'm tempted to make a sexual joke about something being stiff, but not while she's talking about her *mother*. "Isn't he going to be the earl someday?"

"He is, and he takes that responsibility very seriously." She hesitates, offers up a little shrug. "That's why he's so stiff."

Huh. Sounds like George is lots of fun. Sounds like her entire family is fun.

Not really, but hey, I'll try to think positive.

"I don't know when I can get back to England. Not any time soon," I tell her with regret. "We have games scheduled through November and December, and if we make the play-offs, we're playing into January. With practices and travel time, I'm hardly around." I barely have time for myself, let alone anyone else.

Maybe asking her to be my girlfriend was the wrong thing to do...

She sighs, then readjusts herself so she's back under the covers, hiding her delectable body from view. "I should go to bed. I have to work tomorrow."

Notice how she didn't even acknowledge what I said. "How often do you work anyway?"

"It's a part-time job, so only about twenty to twenty-five hours a week, and mostly on Friday and Saturday," she explains, making a little face, like she just smelled something bad.

"You worked today?"

"Yes. It was boring though. I hate my job. But who cares? Not like I'm doing anything with my life anyway." She purses her lips, and I notice how sleepy she looks. I want to ask her more about her job and why she hates it, when she says, "I'll text you tomorrow, okay?"

"Sounds good, babe," I say gently, my entire body aching with the need to touch her. Console her. She seems sad. Restless. I don't like it.

But there's nothing I can do about it.

"Goodnight Susie," I murmur.

"Goodnight." She hits a button and she's gone.

Leaving me alone with my turbulent thoughts for the rest of the night.

TWENTY

SUSANNA

"I CAN'T BELIEVE you're making me do this," Evie grumbles as we climb into her car, both of us slamming the doors quickly so we don't get doused with the endless rain that's been falling the last few days. It's a Saturday morning near the end of November and we're getting a late start, but at least she's going with me, so there is that.

"I need you there for moral support," I tell her as I put on my seatbelt. Leaning back, I watch her until she looks up at me. "You do know how incredibly grateful I am that you're going with me."

More grumbling from Evie as she starts her car. Hers is a beautiful, newer Mercedes Benz, a sporty cream-colored two-door that must have cost a fortune. Her father gave it to her for her last birthday, and thank God she hasn't wrecked it.

Yet.

"I'm even more grateful that you're driving," I continue, staring at the wipers that whip back and forth across the windshield. "You know how I hate traveling in the rain."

"You are like a little old woman, I swear," Evie says with a slight shake of her head. "Wearing your glasses, peering over the steering wheel, complaining when you have to drive in the dark or in the rain."

Her words don't hurt my feelings. She's been complaining about my old woman driving ways for years. "I know you don't want to go either," I say.

"You're right. I don't."

It's because we're going to my parents' estate for the night. More like I've been summoned, and I'm bringing Evie with me to use as defense. Having someone else around tends to make my mother behave better. When I'm alone, she launches into a full scale scolding every single time. If it's not my hair, it's my clothes, or my job, or my choice of friends, or my flat or my lack of a boyfriend or...

Whatever she can find, she will criticize me for it. It's exhausting. And I'm not in the mood to deal with her, especially considering she's not happy about me keeping up my so-called relationship with Cannon.

So-called because truly, we don't see each other. He's so busy, traveling and practicing and doing all of those football things, we rarely talk. We've only FaceTimed twice after that first one where we did such dirty things on camera—I still shudder just thinking about it—and he was so tired both times, we only talked for a few minutes before he ended the calls.

We text a lot though, which is reassuring. I see him on the internet, playing his games. He sent me flowers, once to the gallery, another time to my flat, which was nice. But we haven't had a real face-to-face conversation, haven't talked, haven't done anything that resembles relationship-type stuff in a while.

If I were Evie, I'd say the relationship is doomed.

Before I get too sad over it, I need to change the subject.

"Did I tell you George will be there?" I'm trying to lighten the mood so Evie won't think about my mother—I swear they're mortal enemies, it's so strange—but she whips her head around so fast I'm afraid she might hurt herself, glaring at me when she comes to a stop at a red light.

"Your *brother* will be there this weekend?" Her voice is ice cold, as is the gleam in her dark blue eyes while she continues to stare at me.

"Um..." I'm suddenly nervous. "Yes?"

"I *hate* him." She punches the steering wheel with her fist, wincing like she might've actually hurt herself this time. "Seriously, he's a giant prick, Susanna. If I'd known he was going to be there, I would've said no."

"Oh, come on, George isn't that bad." I don't understand her over-the-top reaction. I know they weren't particularly close, but I didn't think they hated each other. "I thought you two got along." Though they rarely interact.

"He's a total pompous ass. He's always been terrible toward me. He treats me like shit!" She glances around, squirming in her seat. "I could probably turn around here and take you back to your flat—"

"No." I grab her arm, desperation making me do...desperate things. I give her arm a firm shake, like I'm trying to shake some sense into her. "Absolutely not. You're going with me. You *have* to."

"But I don't want to." She jerks her arm out of my hold, giving it a rub, making me feel awful. I probably squeezed too hard. "Come on, Susanna. Don't make me do this."

"You *promised,* Evie. You promised you would go with me." I pause, letting my words hit her hard. "Remember?"

Evie goes still, and then she sighs dramatically, her shoulders drooping, her demeanor slipping into surrender mode. We never back down from a promise to each other. It's the one thing we maintain. Breaking promises would cause sudden death to our friendship.

And neither of us wants to risk that.

"Fine. You're right. I promised." She sounds sad. Yet fierce. "I'll do this, but you owe me."

"Owe you what?" I ask warily. We've had these sorts of conversations before, and I'm always the one who ends up owing her. It's awful, because her demands are never small. She always needs me to bail her out of a sticky situation, no questions asked.

It's the worst.

But she's my best friend, so I'm always there for her, no matter what.

"Whatever I need, whenever I need you, you have to be there." She points a finger at me, her expression one of pure determination. "If I have to suffer this entire weekend with your insufferable family, then I'm going to put you through equal torture. Someday. I *promise.*"

"Fine," I say with an exasperated sigh. I don't know what she could expect of me that would be as torturous as her spending time with my mother and I guess my brother too, but we'll see.

I'm sure Evie can come up with something.

"THERE YOU ARE," my mother coos as Evie and I make our entrance into the house hours later, both of us dripping on the aging rug in the foyer since we got caught in a torrential downpour on our way into the house. Neither of us thought to bring an umbrella, which was stupid. "I was getting worried."

"The rain is terrible," I tell her while I shed my raincoat, as does Evie. My mother's latest maid takes the coats from us, and when I tell her thank you, she curtsies, barely meets my gaze, and then dashes away, like she's scared.

With my mother as her employer, I don't doubt for a minute that she's terrified.

The moment the maid is gone, Mother pulls me into a stiff embrace, her cool cheek pressed against mine for the briefest second before she releases me, though she keeps her hands on my shoulders as her contemplative gaze rakes over me. Assessing my appearance, as per the usual.

"The weather held us up a bit," I tell her.

"Mmm. Hmm. I figured with Evie's mad driving skills, you'd be here *much* sooner." Mother smiles, nodding at Evie, who merely glowers in return.

A compliment wrapped in an insult—that's my mother for you.

"Where's Father?" If he were here, he'd soften the mood a bit. He's so much kinder than my mother, he always has been. Tolerant, fun, and with a keen sense of humor. Patient. Oh, so patient.

He adores Evie, who loves him in return. It's quite touching, how sweet they are to each other.

"He went hunting with the neighbors. He should be back before dinner." Mother clasps her hands together, her gaze going from me to Evie and back to me again. "George should be here soon. And he's bringing a friend."

"A friend?" Evie asks, her voice unnaturally high. I send her a look, but she's solely focused on Mother.

"A young woman he's calling a friend, but I'm hopeful she's more than that." My mother looks like she's going to squeal and bounce in delight, she's so happy at the thought of my brother bringing home a woman he cares about so much, he's willing to let her meet his parents. "Isn't this marvelous news?"

"Marvelous," Evie echoes, hitching her travel bag strap higher onto her shoulder and starting for the stairwell. "Fantastic. Bloody brilliant. I hope George is thrilled to marry the old bag."

Old bag? What in the world?

Evie runs up the stairs before I can say anything, her boots extra loud as they go *stomp, stomp, stomp* up the rattling staircase, and both Mother and I watch her silently until she disappears down the hallway.

"That was—odd," Mother says, sending me a questioning glance. "Why would she act in such a way?"

"I'm not sure." Maybe because she hates George with the fiery passion of a thousand suns? Not that I ever saw them have any sort of interaction where hate could be involved.

Hmm.

Or maybe it's because she's secretly attracted to my brother and is pissed that he's found someone else?

The imaginary lightbulb that suddenly clicks on above my head makes me think it's the latter.

"Well, I don't suppose it matters what your friend thinks. What matters is what your brother's future wife thinks." Mother smiles, and I swear she's the happiest I've seen her in a while. "And I think this young lady sounds promising."

"George has told you about her?" What a surprise, considering he doesn't like to give her any details about his love interests. I don't tell her much either.

"Not really." She smiles. "You know how private he is."

But wait a minute. She hasn't even met this so-called friend yet, and our mother is already calling her George's future wife? "Do you know her name?"

"Lady Priscilla Fischer. Youngest daughter of a marquess." Mother beams. "I did a little investigating. She's a descendant of a German prince. I hear she's distantly related to Prince Albert."

Who's been dead for over one hundred and fifty years. "Wouldn't that make her a distant relative of ours?"

"No, darling, we're related to the queen through Victoria," Mother says with exasperation.

I don't bother reminding her that Victoria and Albert were married and had children, despite the fact that they were first cousins. Nobility doesn't talk about the sordid past, considering it's loaded with various incestuous relationships. She knows this.

She just chooses not to acknowledge it.

"How about you? How are you doing? Still putting on that little charade with the American?" She waves a hand and I dutifully follow her into the sitting room, where a tray laden with a teapot, cups and various frosted cakes awaits us. "Would you like some tea? Perhaps a little snack?"

I join her on the settee, watching as she pours me a cup of tea and adds a dollop of milk. I'm dying for one of those sugary cakes, but she'll probably make a remark about my overly abundant figure and how I should watch my weight.

I don't want to hear it, so I don't reach for a snack. I'll sneak a cake later, from the kitchen.

"Well?" she asks once she's handed me over the cup and I still haven't answered. "Are you still involved in your little relationship with him?" Her nose wrinkles at the word *relationship*.

And now *my* nose is wrinkling, remembering how she called our relationship a charade only a moment ago. Only I would let something like that fly by and not even acknowledge it. She's so cruel sometimes, and the saddest thing is that I'm used to her behavior.

"Yes, we are," I say coolly, wishing for about the hundredth time that Cannon could come back to England and meet my parents in an official manner.

My mother sets her cup and saucer on the table in front of us with a loud clank. "Susanna, really. When are you going to stop pretending you could have something with this man and concentrate on your reality?"

Her words make me sit up straighter, automatically going on the defensive. "Cannon *is* my reality," I insist, though I'm secretly starting to have more and more doubts as the days slip by and I don't really talk to him.

Not that I can ever admit that to her. My mother would jump on that knowledge and convince me to end things with him by Sunday afternoon. She still wields that much power over me.

Does that make me weak?

When it comes to my mother, yes. I suppose it does.

"He's stringing you along. I don't think he knows how to end this silly dalliance. He's afraid he'll hurt your feelings," she says, like she has so much knowledge about Cannon and how he thinks.

"You don't even know him," I protest, and she silences me with a look.

"I know men like him. They're all the same." She sips from her cup, staring at me from over the rim of her fine bone china. My eyes are the same shade as hers, icy and cold when they want to be. "He most likely wants to let you down easy."

This is a familiar argument. One we've had before. Maybe I should say something different to distract her.

"Perhaps he'll try to ghost me," I tell her, and she frowns.

She frowns. "What exactly does that mean?"

I love it when I can tell her something she doesn't understand. Petty, yes, but oh so satisfying.

"When someone just stops calling you, texting you, seeing you, whatever. They just vanish from your life one day with no warning, no explanation. Like a ghost. Poof." I snap my fingers for emphasis.

"Ah. That does make sense." She nods, and I know she's storing that info into her brain to pull out later. Maybe she'll use it on George and surprise him that she even knows such a thing. "He could do that to you, darling. Just one day stop talking to you."

I can't imagine sweet, thoughtful Cannon ghosting me, but who knows? I only spent a few days with him. I have no idea who he really is, or what he thinks. Or truly what he wants. "I think he'd have the courtesy to at least tell me it's not going to work out between us."

"Courtesy." Mom sniffs, like I said an unfamiliar word. "Who's courteous anymore? No young people I know. You're all too busy playing on your phones or chatting on social media, or acting like you know better than everyone else."

Ah, my mother's favorite thing is to act like *she* knows better than everyone else. I rarely do that to her, and she knows it. That's why it's always so easy for her to push me around and tell me what to do.

I'm about to say something, protest her generalizing my generation and whatnot, when my brother suddenly enters the sitting room, holding hands with a tall, beautiful woman who looks like a model.

"Mother, Susanna." His rich, deep voice is the slightest bit shaky, and I know he's nervous. "How are you?"

"George, my darling!" Mother leaps to her feet and practically runs to him, pulling him into an embrace and forcing him to let go of his new girlfriend's hand.

Reminding good ol' Lady Priscilla that she will always come second in his life if Mother has anything to say about it.

"Such an enthusiastic greeting." George laughs nervously, pulling out of her embrace. He returns to Priscilla's side, resting his hand at the small of her back and guiding her toward us. "Mother, I want to introduce you to Lady Priscilla Fischer."

"Priscilla. It is so lovely to meet you." Mother takes her hand and holds it, as if she's waiting for Priscilla to curtsy. But she doesn't, of course. My mother isn't the queen, though she does believe she's the queen of her castle.

God, I wish Evie were here right now, watching this unfold. She would be laughing her arse off.

"And this is my sister," George says after Mother and Priscilla are done with their pleasantries. "Susanna, this is Priscilla."

"I'm so happy to meet you," Priscilla says as she enthusiastically shakes my hand. Her smile is wide, her teeth blindingly white. "George has told me *so* much about you."

A blank smile appears on my face. I wish I could say the same about her, but I can't. George hasn't mentioned her at all. "It's lovely to meet you. I'm glad you were able to join us this weekend."

"Oh, me too! I'm thrilled to be able to celebrate your parents' wedding anniversary with the family," Priscilla says.

Wait, it's their anniversary weekend? How could I forget? Oh, I'm sure my mother is absolutely furious at my father that he's out hunting in the rain with the neighbors, instead of spending time with her.

This ought to make for an interesting couple of days.

TWENTY-ONE
SUSANNA

"YOU MUST GIVE ME EVERY DETAIL," Evie says the moment I enter the bedroom we're sharing. She refuses to sleep anywhere but in my childhood room, and thankfully I have two double beds. She firmly believes my family's estate is haunted, and it might very well be, though the ghosts tend to leave me alone.

"Every detail about what?" I ask as I quietly shut the door behind me. I'd planned on trying to take a nap, but from the current state Evie seems to be in, I can tell my nap plans will have to wait.

Evie's hair is sticking up every which way, like she's clawed her fingers through it the entire time I've been downstairs with Mother, and her eyes are a little wild, darting here and there as she nervously chews on her lower lip. If I didn't know her better, I'd almost wonder if she was having some sort of anxiety attack. Or perhaps a seizure.

She's looking quite unhinged.

"Every detail about your brother's new girlfriend, of course." The tone of her voice is one big *duh*, like I should know what she's asking for. "What's she like?"

"She's very nice," I say as I grab my duffel bag from the floor and throw it on my bed, unzipping it so I can pull out the black cardigan I packed. The old house is drafty, and the bedroom wing in particular is extra cold.

"Very *nice?* That's it? That's all you can say?" she asks incredulously.

I turn to face her. Evie's standing in front of me with her hands on her hips and a hostile expression on her face. Clearly my earlier suspicions are more than confirmed. I'm fairly certain my best friend has a—a *thing* for my older brother.

When in the world did this happen?

"George seems quite taken with her," I say, purposely trying to drive her crazy, which is cruel of me, but please. She can't be with George. He's my brother. What if it doesn't work out? I don't want to be caught in the middle of their sordid affair, because that's all it would end up being.

A sordid affair. Most definitely.

My mother wouldn't allow it either. She hates Evie. And Evie hates her. Why in the world would she want to be with my older brother when he is constantly seeking the approval of our mother, a woman she absolutely cannot stand?

"Of course he's taken. She's absolutely beautiful. Stunning even," Evie says, her voice low, and when I send her a sharp look, she shrugs helplessly. "I spied on you all in the sitting room."

"Peeking through the cracks of the doors?" I ask jokingly.

"Yes, that's exactly what I did." She starts pacing the room, running her fingers through her hair and tugging on the ends in seeming frustration. "She looks like a fucking model," she practically wails.

My exact thought. "She *is* rather tall."

"And gorgeous!"

"Like a model," I agree.

Evie literally growls, her eyes flashing with anger when she stops to look at me. "You're making this worse, you know."

"How? By agreeing with you that my brother's girlfriend is gorgeous? What's the big deal anyway, huh, Evie? Why do you care what George is doing or who he's with? You're not making much sense right now."

She completely ignores my questions. "Do you think George is in love with her?"

"If he's willing to bring her to meet our parents during their anniversary weekend, then yes. I do believe he is completely in love with her," I say with total honesty.

"Oh God." Evie makes her way to her bed, throwing herself on it like a lovesick teenage girl, lying on her stomach with her face buried in the pillow. "I can't believe it," she wails, her voice muffled.

"Evie." I walk over to her bed and grab her arm, forcing her to turn so she has to look at me. "What in the world is wrong with you?"

She's crying. Tough-as-nails, never-takes-any-shit, will-do-anything-to-help-me Evie, is helplessly sobbing right now. "It's George."

"What about George?"

"I think—" She takes a heaving breath, a little hiccup escaping her when she exhales. "No, I'm fairly certain that I'm in love with him."

I gape at her. *No*. Crushing on him? Sure. Feel a minor attraction toward him? That's fine. Acceptable.

In love with George?

I think not.

"How in the world are you in love with him? You two literally never speak to each other. Ever," I say, pausing when I see the guilt flash in her eyes. "Are you two keeping something from me?"

Evie sits up, her gaze imploring as she watches me. "We... we've hooked up a few times, me and George."

"Huh?" I'm not able to comprehend what she's saying. "How?"

"Do I really need to describe how two adults hook up, Susanna?" Ah, there's the sarcastic Evie I know and love.

"Of course not! Just...tell me how you two even crossed paths. I only thought you ever saw him when you were with me," I say.

"You're right. I've only ever spent time with him when I'm with you or your family. I never even really thought about George, you know? He was just there," Evie admits.

It's true. George could be like a shadow man sometimes. Always around, someone to count on being there, even if you never spoke to him. He's quiet, like our father. Thoughtful. Patient. Again, like my father. Handsome, I suppose, though I'm not one to rattle on and on about my brother's looks. He takes more after Father, with the rich brown hair that can flop in his eyes sometimes and a distinctive nose. Rather tall, over six feet, and lanky. He likes to run and cycle. A bit of a health nut, when I'd rather indulge in sweets. I don't exercise at all, though I know I should...

"...so I ran into him at a bar a few months ago. Some place that big-wig bankers hang out at, you know? The sort of place that's dark and sleek and modern, and full of well-dressed blokes with their ties half undone and their hair a mess and eyes bleary after working ten hours straight staring at a computer screen," Evie explains.

"You go to those sorts of places?" I ask dazedly.

"I *live* for those sorts of places. All of those uptight business gents looking to unwind. They're usually full of passion," Evie says.

I do not want to think about my big brother being *full of passion*.

"Anyway, I'm at one of those bars and I run into George. He's with a group of friends and he invites me to join them," she continues.

"Wait a minute," I say, interrupting her. "Were you alone?"

She shrugs and looks away.

"Evie," I draw out her name like I do when I'm chastising her for doing something risky. "You shouldn't go to the bars alone."

"You were busy, going on a date with some asshole," she mutters, her description most accurate. Lately everyone I've gone on a date with has been an asshole—with the exception of Cannon. "I had no one else to hang out with, and I wanted to let loose and have some fun."

My heart breaks a little at thinking of Evie lonely, and me not being there for her. She must see it on my face, too.

Evie waves a hand, dismissing my worry. "Please. I'm fine. I found George, and he of course chastised me for being at a bar alone."

Pride fills me at thinking of George giving Evie a hard time about her poor life choices. Us Sumners do look out for our friends' safety.

"He started by scolding me like an old man, and I taunted him like a naughty girl, but after we grew tired of that façade, we started having a real conversation. He asked me questions. He actually seemed to—care." She blinks at me, appearing a little dazzled. "I ended up talking with George for the rest of the night. His friends eventually abandoned him, and the bar slowly emptied out, until we were the last two sitting there, still engrossed in conversation. When we realized they were hoping to close up, he suggested we go have a late dinner together, and I agreed because I was starving."

"Okay," I say, intrigued. "Go on."

"We went to one restaurant not far from my place, but it was terribly crowded, and the wait was endless. We ended up going to another restaurant, a tiny little Asian place that had the most delicious food I've ever eaten. We shared plates, we sat close to each other, all cozy and a little drunk, and the next thing I knew, his hand was on my knee. He didn't seem in a hurry to remove it, and the weirdest thing was, I actually *wanted* him to touch me."

Oh no. "Are you going to go into more detail?" I wince, needing to stop this conversation if she does.

"Do you not want to hear all the details?" Evie asks, her expression pure innocence.

"Not about my brother," I say vehemently, making her laugh.

"I won't go into *full* detail, but we ended up going back to my flat that night and...hooking up."

I almost want to stick my fingers in my ears and chant gibberish to ward off her words. "God, did you two have—"

"Sex? Not that night," she admits.

"Oh my God, you've had sex with my brother!" I practically shriek.

Evie climbs off the bed, clasping her hand over my mouth. "Shush! They might hear you!"

"So? They *should* hear you! God, you've gotten naked with my brother and now he's here with his new lady friend and what he's doing is so *wrong*, Evie. Having the both of you here is going to muck things up very, very badly."

The understatement of the year.

My head feels as if it's literally spinning at her confession. If George has had sex with my best friend, then why did he bring Priscilla here? Is she really his girlfriend? Is this some sort of game he's playing?

"I don't understand what's happening," I say, voicing my concern. And confusion. I rub my temples with my fingers. "This makes no sense."

"You're right. It makes absolutely no sense. And I know my being here with George and his new—girlfriend mucks everything up. This is why I didn't want to come." She points a finger at me. "I told you I didn't want to be here. You should've listened to me."

I should've. I so should've.

Taking a deep breath, I try to assess the situation logically. "Okay. So you've had sex with George. Big deal, right? It's nothing serious between you two."

She's quiet. Too quiet. I don't like this.

"I've had sex with your brother multiple times," she finally says.

I'm frowning so hard my forehead hurts. "Multiple?"

She nods.

"When you say multiple, do you mean more than twice?"

"Oh yes," she says with enthusiasm.

Too much enthusiasm.

"At least—ten times?" That sounds extreme, but when I count how many times Cannon and I had actual sex when he was here, it was at least ten times. Perhaps more.

She nods again.

I close my eyes. Take a deep breath. Count to ten before I open them again. "When was the last time you had sex with George?"

"Hmm, last week, maybe?" She throws her hands up in the air. "Yes, definitely last week. I don't know why I'm being coy."

"Are you *serious?*" I'm screeching, but I can't help it. This is all just so scandalous. "Then why is he bringing Lady Priscilla to the house and not you?"

"He knows your mother will flip her shit if he ever brought me around as his girlfriend! Besides, he doesn't call me his girlfriend. He claims we have an understanding," Evie says, making air quotes with her fingers.

"Oh, that understanding thing is complete and utter shit, and you know it! How dare he?" Now I'm pissed at George on Evie's behalf.

"It's what I thought I wanted too. You know how I don't like labels," she says, and she's right. I do know how much she hates labels. She doesn't want to be just any one thing.

Evie's always wanted to be *all* the things.

"Right, but he's not acknowledging that the two of you have a relationship," I explain, hoping that she realizes just how much of a jerk George is being.

"It's not a relationship. He's not my boyfriend. It *is* an understanding. We're doing it just for the sex," she insists, but her eyes are starting to well up with tears again, and I'm afraid there's more than sex involved here.

Sounds like there are honest to goodness feelings.

And I'm afraid Evie's going to end up with a broken heart.

TWENTY-TWO

SUSANNA

I'M GETTING ready for dinner when my phone rings with a FaceTime call from Cannon. I rush to grab my phone, terrified I'll miss the call and then I'll be unable to get a hold of him, and when his handsome face fills my screen, my heart trips over itself in happiness.

"Cannon," I say breathlessly.

"Susie," he returns with a big grin. "You look beautiful."

Now my heart swells to three times its size. "Why thank you. I'm getting ready for dinner."

"Where are you?"

"My parents' house, remember? Evie and I are here for the weekend." I switch the angle of the camera so he can see the room. "This is my old bedroom. Evie and I are sharing it."

"Where is she at?"

I flip the phone camera back around so it's on my face once again. "Taking a shower." She just got in, after I spent at least thirty minutes trying to convince her that yes, she absolutely has to come down for dinner tonight, or it would look weird. And her not appearing would give George the sense that he won.

I'm not going to let him win this. No way.

"So you're all alone?" Cannon raises his brows, his expression darkening.

"Yes, but I'm not going to dirty talk with you or expose myself. Not here," I tell him primly, making him laugh.

"I wasn't going to ask you to do any of that stuff, though I do miss you and wouldn't mind seeing that pretty little body of yours," he says longingly.

My skin goes warm at his sweet words. "We should set up another video date."

"We should." He takes a deep breath, exhaling loudly before he announces, "I got hurt yesterday."

"Wait, what? What do you mean?" Now my heart is racing. This man puts me through all the emotions in a short amount of time, and it's almost too much to handle.

"I was at practice, running on the field and I don't know, my knee just—gave out." He shrugs. "Hurts like a bitch."

"No one tackled you or anything?" I still don't know much about American football or how it works. I try to watch his games, but most of them aren't broadcasted here, so it's quite difficult.

"No, I was by myself. Well, I wasn't by myself, but no one else was around me when it happened. I had trouble with my knee back in high school, and even had to have surgery the summer after my sophomore year. But I thought it was fixed. Never gave me any problems until now," he says.

"Where are you? Are you at home?" Hmm, I don't think so. None of his surroundings look familiar.

"I'm in a hotel room. In Arizona. We play the Cardinals tomorrow."

"Are you playing in the game?"

"I want to, but I don't know if they're going to let me." He looks so sad, so disappointed, and I wish I were actually there to comfort him.

"I'm sure they'll let you play," I say, my voice falsely bright. "You'll feel better tomorrow, I'm sure of it. Did they give you anything to help with the pain?"

"Oh yeah, I'm wearing a brace and they gave me a cortisone shot, plus some painkillers, though I really don't want to use them. My knee is swollen, and they said they're going to get me in for an X-ray or a CT scan tomorrow or Monday. I don't know." The frustration is clear in his voice, on his face. "I just don't want this injury to end my career."

Fear makes my voice tremble. "Is it that bad?"

"They're thinking it could be pretty bad," he admits.

I feel like he's putting on a brave face so I won't worry. He's telling me the things he wants me to hear, what he wants to believe, but it's not the whole truth.

"I wish I was there with you," I whisper.

He smiles, though it doesn't quite reach his eyes, which tells me he's extremely worried. "I wish you were too. Though I don't think there's much you could do for me."

"I could rub your shoulders. Fix you your favorite foods," I suggest.

"You can cook?"

I wrinkle my nose. "Not really."

He laughs, and the sound eases my worry. I love it when he laughs. "You really can't cook, Susie?"

"Not particularly. My mother never taught me how, because we have cooks on staff," I say.

"Just how rich are you?"

I never did divulge much about my family's financial status. "We're one of those rare nobility lines that actually has money versus just a title and a crumbling estate. The Sumner men have worked in finance for generations," I tell him. "They invest wisely."

"So that makes you worth some money."

"We have some money, yes."

"That's why you only work part-time."

"It was a volunteer job at first," I admit, making him chuckle. "What, it's true! I've always loved art, and was an art history major in college."

"Did you graduate?"

"No." I feel a little helpless at admitting this. "I haven't accomplished much in life." I sound morose, only because

I'm ashamed. He's done so much with his life in such a short amount of time and I've done...

Absolutely nothing.

"Hey, don't be down on yourself. I think you're pretty awesome." He smiles, and seeing it brightens my whole mood.

"Thank you. Here you are injured and worried and you're trying to make me feel better," I say, feeling awful. I didn't mean to turn this around on me.

"It's what I do." He leans in so I can see his face even better, and I'm filled with the need to kiss him. That he's thousands of miles away is a true obstacle. "How are your parents?"

"It's their thirtieth wedding anniversary tonight," I say. "And I forgot."

"You didn't bring them a gift?"

"No, I did not. I am their gift. The gift that keeps on giving."

"I'd like to think you're my gift," he says, his voice dipping low, his eyes getting that sleepy, sexy look I know and love.

Love. The word keeps popping up in my thoughts, and I should be a little startled by that, right?

But I'm not.

"You're definitely my gift," I return, my voice soft, my heart fluttering from the admission. "And this weekend is going to be interesting. There's so much I already have to tell you."

"Tell me now."

I hear the shower water shut off down the hall—yes, the walls are extremely thin—and know I don't have much time before Evie's back in the room. And then I can't tell Cannon anything. "How about I call you tomorrow, when I return from my parents' place?"

"I'll call you. I have the game tomorrow, and it could be hectic." He hesitates, a frown curling his perfectly sexy lips. "Though by the time I'm through with everything, you might be asleep."

"Call me anyway. I want to talk to you." I smile, the corners trembling as I'm suddenly overcome with emotion. "I miss you. So much."

"I miss you too, baby." He sighs. Runs a hand through his hair. "Send me good luck vibes for tomorrow. I need them."

"I will. I promise."

TWENTY-THREE

CANNON

I LIED TO SUSANNA. I haven't lied to a woman in years —it's something I don't like to do. But when I was in high school, I could be kind of a jackass, and I went through a player stage, working my way through the girls at school like they were disposable. One after another after another. And when a guy goes through a player stage, especially a teen asshole with a chip on his shoulder like me, he tends to lie.

A lot.

Em, my first serious girlfriend, wouldn't tolerate my lies. She warned me when we first got together. She taught me that liars are the absolute worst. Deep down, I always knew she was right, but I lied to her anyway, about something stupid and inconsequential, and she about lost her shit.

I never lied to her again. I never lied to *any* woman again.

Until today. With Susanna.

And I feel guilty as shit about it, too.

Sighing, I run my hands through my hair, tugging on the ends, glaring at the black brace wrapped tightly around my knee. I definitely got hurt in practice yesterday, and they already told me I'm not allowed to play tomorrow. I'm stuck here in Arizona with a bum knee and a shitty attitude, and no one wants to be around me. Not even Jordan, who's my best friend. I about bit his head off earlier, when they were escorting me off the field during practice and he asked what's wrong.

That's it. All he did was ask me what was wrong, and I yelled at him like he just kicked my dog and stole my girlfriend.

I am a complete jackass.

Our coaches let me get away with it, because they knew I was in pain and frustrated and scared. Not that any of us big burly men like to admit that, but yeah. Fuck yeah. I was terrified.

I'm still terrified.

I've been to the doctor. They did an X-ray. I have a torn meniscus. I'm lucky I didn't tear my ACL, but I did serious damage, and I've done this sort of thing before. Because of the previous injury, the team doctor had a firm suggestion.

I'm out for the season.

And fuck, that hurts so damn much, I don't know how to deal with it. So I lashed out.

Oh, and I lie.

Football is *everything* to me. It's my life. It's been my life for almost as long as I can remember, and I've let it consume me these last few years, since I became a professional. I have one shot at this, and I know it. The sport is rough, it will take you out in a split second, without warning, and right now, I feel like I've lost my dream.

My entire career.

It's not a career-ending injury, the doctors and my coaches insist. *Season-ending, yes. But you'll play next year,* they tell me. *You might need surgery, you'll do physical therapy, and you'll be back at it in no time.*

Their words offer little reassurance, not with the constant doubt running through my head. They can't one hundred percent guarantee I'll be "back at it in no time." They don't know shit. This injury could be worse than they think. I might not recover fast enough. I'm not getting any younger, and there are hungry, young, strong-as-hell players coming up behind me, dying to take my place.

I don't know what I'd do if I had to give up my spot on the team.

Where would I go? What would I do with my life? I have money, yeah, and I'm under contract, so they'd have to finish paying me even if I couldn't play any longer.

But I'm young. I don't have a plan for after football. Well, I sort of do, but I'm not ready for it yet. I don't want to go out like this, not now.

I'll be fine, I tell myself when I'm trying to be positive. Maybe everyone's right. This isn't career-ending, only season-ending. And shit, the season was almost over anyway. We're going to the playoffs, and we could possibly go all the way to the Super Bowl, but I don't know. Nothing's guaranteed.

Honestly? I don't want them to get to the Super Bowl because I can't play in it. And that is the most selfish feeling I've ever experienced.

So I lied to Susanna because I can't admit that my chances at losing my career are staring me right in the face. And what if she loses interest in me once she finds out I can't play football anymore? I don't think she's shallow like that, but I don't know. Maybe I'd become too much trouble.

A burden.

I can barely stomach the thought.

I'm trying to keep up the pretense that everything's going to be fine, when I have no clue if it's going to be fine or not. It looks to me like it could be over.

But I don't know.

I do know that I miss Susanna. And I already miss football.

I'm strong, but I'm scared.

And that's the hardest part to admit.

TWENTY-FOUR

SUSANNA

THE TENSION in the dining room is so thick, you can cut it with a knife.

I always thought that saying was silly. Unbelievable. But I've never experienced such tension before, and now I understand how the saying came about.

Because it's true. The tension between everyone tonight is off the charts. My parents—Mother is angry at Father for essentially spending their anniversary with our neighbors instead of her. George is scared Evie is going to blow his cover about their secret affair so he won't even look in her direction. Evie is dying to blurt out that she's been messing around with George in secret, yet she's also chatting up Priscilla, and oh my God, I believe she actually likes the supermodel.

Not that Priscilla is an *actual* supermodel. She's gorgeous, and it turns out she's one of those YouTube vlogger types who does makeup tutorials and has scads of followers. This fascinates Evie, so she keeps engaging in conversation with her, trying to find out how she became popular on YouTube, and it's *killing* George. He looks so tense, like he might shatter if anyone so much as looks at him wrong.

Me? I'm feeling no tension. Not really. Well, my mother is upset with me for some reason. Perhaps she just hates the way I breathe, but I'm used to that, so no worries. Father is keeping up conversation with me, because I'm the only one who'll talk to him. Mother's too angry with his neglect, and the rest of them are too preoccupied with their own issues.

I'm preoccupied as well, though I'm doing a good job faking it. I can't stop thinking about Cannon and his knee injury.

Is he really all right? Was he putting on a brave face for me, and is he dealing with a situation that is far more serious than he's letting on?

I'm starting to think that's it. It's worse than he wants to confess, and why he would keep something from me like that, I'm not sure, but he has to know that I'll be there for him no matter what.

Or maybe he doesn't know. We're still practically strangers. I haven't had a chance to prove myself yet. Maybe he's realizing our relationship would be so much easier if I were an American who lives in California. It's so difficult for us to be there for each other when we live so far away.

"Mother says you're dating a professional football player," George says, his inquisitive voice pulling me from my thoughts. "Is that true, Susanna?"

I blink my brother into focus, see the fake smile on his face. I think he's trying to change the subject, and using me in the process.

Great.

I decide to go along with it, and help ease his pain.

"It's true. I met him a few weeks ago," I say with a nod.

"The giant young man we met the weekend of that exhibition game?" Father pipes up, surprise in his voice.

"Yes, Father, you remember him?" I turn to smile at my father, ignoring the glare coming from my mother.

"I do. Nice fellow. Rather large." That's all he can ever seem to say about Cannon, which I suppose is normal, considering Cannon *is* unusually huge.

"Darling, you should've spoken to him longer, so you could've come home and given me a report," Mother says, her voice shrill as she studies my father. "Now our daughter is dating someone we don't even know. Someone who doesn't even live in this country."

Evie sends me a helpless look, but doesn't say anything. I'm sure she's glad the attention is off her as well.

"What team does he play for?" Priscilla asks, her soft voice startling me for a moment.

"The San Francisco 49ers," I tell her with a little smile.

"Oh." She tilts her head. "So he's not an actual footballer."

"He's an *American* footballer," Evie adds.

"Well, that's exciting!" Priscilla claps her hands together. "And he's from California. Oh, you must go visit him and watch one of his games sometime, don't you think? How exciting would that be?"

I like her enthusiasm. It's refreshing.

"She can't just pick up and leave," Mother says, sending me a knowing look.

"Why not?" Evie asks, her tone innocent. Her question anything but.

"She has responsibilities, and a life here. To put it in complete upheaval for a man she hardly knows is...*ridiculous*. Besides, California is so dreadfully far," Mother says. "And Susanna has never traveled alone before. She wouldn't know what to do with herself."

Ouch. Thanks for all your faith in me, Mother.

"Maybe I could go with her," Evie suggests, making Mother laugh.

"I don't think so," Mother says with finality.

"Over my dead body," George adds, his enraged tone startling everyone.

Especially Evie.

"Why do you care?" Her tone is snippy.

"You can't travel all the way to California by yourself," George says, all blustery and protective. "Something could happen to you."

"But I'd be with Susanna," Evie starts, but he shakes his head, cutting her off.

"The two of you traveling alone is dangerous. I forbid it," George says.

He *forbids* it? Oh dear, Evie is going to lose it.

"Who do you think you are?" Evie grabs the cloth napkin from her lap and tosses it onto her still mostly full plate. She rises to her feet, glaring at my brother. "You can't tell me what to do."

"Like hell I can't." George stands, the two of them having a furious faceoff across the table from each other.

My mouth hangs open as I watch the drama unfold. Father appears confused, as does poor, innocent Priscilla. Mother, though, she's taking in this shit show before her with absolute disgust.

"What in the world are you two doing?" she asks, her voice calm, the look in her eyes anything but. "Sit down. Now."

"No," Evie and George say in unison.

"Evie," I whisper, suddenly worried for the fate of my older brother and only heir to the Harwood estate. Mother looks ready to wrench his head from his neck. No one ever tells her no. Evie might be banned from any family function for life. "You should probably sit down. Or maybe even...leave the room until you can cool off?"

She doesn't respond, doesn't even look at me. She's too busy glaring at my brother, and he's glaring at her in return. They remain quiet for so long, everyone starts to squirm in their seat.

Well, I'm squirming in my seat, at least. I don't know about everyone else.

Finally, *finally* George breaks the silence first.

"I don't want to cool off," he says, his tone firm, his eyes blazing as he stares at Evie.

Blazing with...passion?

Oh my.

Priscilla appears totally confused, and Evie keeps blinking, like she might be trying to stop herself from crying.

"I should go," she finally says, her voice cracking.

But she doesn't move.

"Please don't go," George says quietly. "I have—I have something to confess."

No one says anything. Not even Mother, which is unlike her. Until...

"What is it, George?" Evie asks.

She knows his confession is for her.

He turns to look at the woman he brought with him for the weekend, his expression contrite. "Priscilla, I'm terribly sorry for wasting your time, but I'm afraid I must tell you something," he says, his voice soft, his gaze still locked on Evie. "I have—feelings for someone else."

Evie blinks yet again, surprise etched in her fine features. "You do?" she asks, her voice weak.

George nods. "I'm an utter fool, Evie. Can you forgive me?"

Wait a minute. Is my brother...

"Yes." Evie is full-on crying now. Again. "Oh, George."

"Please, Evie." He's actually begging.

"I forgive you," she sobs. "Of course I forgive you."

"I'm in love with you." George laughs. Shakes his head. "I have a funny way of showing it, bringing another woman here to my parents' home, but I think I was trying to convince myself to do the right thing, when the right thing—the *only* thing—was in front of me the entire time."

Aww. That is the most romantic thing I've ever heard my brother—or pretty much anyone—ever say.

"George, what in the world are you doing?" Mother's sharp voice nearly makes me jump out of my chair.

George sends her a quick glance. "I'm saying that I'm in love with Evie and I want to be with her."

If I could've whipped my phone out and snapped a photo of the shocked expression on our mother's face when George told her that, it would've been worth me getting yelled at. But alas, I'm too slow, and missed the opportunity. And Mother is extremely skilled at smoothing out her expression in a matter of seconds to make it seem like whatever she was just told doesn't bother her.

But this admission bothers her profusely. I know it does. She cannot stand Evie. My best friend.

Now the love of my brother's life.

"You want to be with me?" Evie squeaks. "Oh my God."

She dashes around the table and grabs George, pulling him in for a hug. My brother embraces her, holding her close, then slips his fingers beneath her chin and kisses her for so long, I finally have to look away.

Seeing them confess their love for each other makes me miss Cannon. Makes me miss his smile and his voice and his touch and his kisses.

Long-distance relationships are the absolute worst.

My gaze snags on Priscilla's and she smiles at me, a little sadly. Everyone around the table seems to go wild at once. Mother's yelling, Father's asking Priscilla if she needs a ride home, Evie is beaming from ear to ear, and I go to Priscilla, take her hand and pull her out of the dining room, away from the chaos.

"I am so sorry," I start, but Priscilla cuts me off with a shake of her head, a serene smile curling her lips.

"It's fine. I had a feeling he was interested in someone else all along," she says.

I'm frowning. "How did you know?"

"Call it womanly instinct." Priscilla actually laughs. "We don't really know each other that well. We're work mates, and we have mutual friends."

"Wait." I frown at her. "I thought you were a YouTuber."

"Oh, I do that too." She waves a hand, smiling. "But I also work in finance. Anyway. One of our friends suggested George and I should go out on a date, and so we did."

"When?" I ask.

"Last Friday."

"So you've only been dating him for a week?" My brows shoot up, I can't help it.

Didn't she think it suspect George wanted to bring her round to meet the parents so soon? Talk about a red flag.

"If you can call one date and a request to accompany him to his parents' house for the weekend as dating, then yes," Priscilla answers.

Oh. My. God. My brother did all of this *on purpose*. He had to! He used this poor woman to what…somehow get back at Evie? Make her jealous? I don't know the full story here, and I'm not sure if I ever will, but I do know that I feel terribly sorry for Priscilla and her part in all of this.

"You must hate my brother," I say. "And you're allowed to. He's kind of a prick." He's a *total* prick.

"No, I don't hate him. Not at all. He was just confused." She smiles, but it's tinged with sadness. I wonder if she's trying to put up a brave front. I mean, if I were her, I wouldn't confess anything to me either. I'm his sister, after all.

Father appears in the corridor, blinking rapidly when he finds us. "Priscilla, dear, I've arranged for a taxi to come pick you up. It should be here in twenty-five minutes."

Calling for a taxi in the country is never a quick process.

"A taxi, Dad? Won't that cost a fortune by the time she gets to London?"

"I'm covering it," he says with a wave of his hand. "And I'll force George to pay me back later."

We all laugh at that one.

"I can drive her back," I suggest.

"You absolutely cannot," Priscilla says at the same time my father says, "Brilliant idea! I'll cancel the taxi."

He's gone in an instant, pulling his cell phone out of his pocket as he walks away.

"You don't need to drive me," Priscilla says when he's gone. "I can take that taxi, and I'll even pay for it."

"Please, I'll drive you. I want out of here anyway," I tell her. "Just let me go gather my things, and I'll be ready in a few minutes."

"Are you sure?" Priscilla's frowning. "You want to take a car ride with the woman your brother just rejected for your best friend?"

"More like do you want to spend an entire car ride to London with the sister of the man who just rejected you for *her* best friend?" I return.

Priscilla laughs. "I don't have a problem with it if you don't."

"I don't," I tell her with a smile.

"I need to pack as well," she says, and it's decided for us.

"Meet me in the foyer then, and off we'll go." I give her arm a reassuring pat and return to the dining room to let everyone know I'm leaving with Priscilla.

Not that anyone is really paying attention. George and Evie are engrossed in an intimate conversation, constantly touching each other, while Dad is yelling into his phone at the taxi company, and Mother is watching the newly declared couple with undisguised disgust.

"I'm definitely taking Priscilla home," I tell my father once he's finished with his call. "So I won't be returning."

"Aw, my sweet, I didn't get to see you much." Dad smiles at me and I wrap him up in a big hug.

"I'll come back another time. Or maybe you can visit me in the city." I lean in close to his ear to murmur, "Maybe you can leave Mother at home."

He laughs and shakes his head. "That actually sounds quite nice."

I approach George and Evie next, slapping my brother hard on the arm and making him yelp. "You should be ashamed of yourself."

"Why?" he asks incredulously as he turns to face me.

"Bringing Priscilla here when you're not interested in her and torturing Evie. How dare you!"

Evie slips her arm around his waist and snuggles up close to him. "Love makes people do stupid things." She doesn't seem the slightest bit angry with him. No, more like she appears blissfully in love with my sod of a brother.

"I hope you two are very happy together," I say sincerely. And I do wish that for the both of them, despite my reservation at them actually working out. They seem like such opposites.

But maybe that's what helps them get along. They balance each other out. Cannon and I are very different, and perhaps that's to our advantage. Look at my parents. My father and mother are nothing alike, yet they've been married a long time. And they seem relatively happy.

Well. Sort of.

"I hear you're driving Priscilla back to London?" George asks with brotherly concern. "It's raining, you know. And it's dark."

He also knows how I don't like to drive in the dark or during bad weather. The combination really sends me over the edge.

But for some reason, tonight I feel brave.

Oh, and then there's the fact that I want the hell out of here.

"And what vehicle are you going to use?" he continues. "One of Dad's cars?"

"You can drive my car," Evie suggests.

My mouth drops open at her offer. "You're going to let me drive the fancy Mercedes your father gave you?"

"Do you have a spare pair of driving glasses?" she asks.

"I do," I reassure her. "I keep a pair in my bedroom, just in case." The prescription might be old, but they should work. Shouldn't they?

"Okay. Just...please don't wreck the car. My father will kill me." Evie disentangles herself from my brother and moves so she's standing next to me. "It's the least I can do after what just happened."

"Priscilla seems all right," I say. "If you were worried about her."

I'm guessing from the look on Evie's face that Priscilla really didn't even cross her mind. "I'm glad. I didn't want her to get her feelings hurt."

"That's for my brother to worry about, not you." I grab her and pull her in for a quick hug. "I'm happy for you. If this is really what you want."

"It is," she murmurs just before she kisses me on the cheek. "I want to be with George. I just hope you're not angry with me. Or with him too."

"I'm not angry." I pull away from her so I can meet her gaze. "I'm just...it's weird? You and George? I can't imagine it."

"Well, imagine it. Because it's true." She sends a quick, worried look in Mother's direction before she returns her attention to me. "That's the one who scares me."

"You should be scared. She might try to destroy your relationship." Is it wrong I'm a little happy that my brother's newfound relationship with Evie will take some of Mother's focus off me? That's selfish of me to think, but it's the truth.

Maybe she'll finally leave me alone now.

Ha. I could be so lucky.

TWENTY-FIVE

CANNON

I'M SITTING around sulking in my hotel room when I get the first phone call from Susanna around one o'clock in the afternoon.

"Hey, baby," I answer wearily, still depressed over my fucked-up knee and fucked-up life, but there's no response.

Just dead air. A loud click, then nothing.

Huh.

I receive a couple more calls just like it, and they worry me. To the point that I send her a quick text.

You okay? I keep receiving calls from your number, but I can't hear you.

Ten, twenty, thirty minutes later, and still no response.

I try calling. Nothing. I keep trying, until her phone gets to the point that it doesn't even ring anymore. Just goes straight to voicemail and her lilting, almost snooty accented voice says:

Hello, you've reached the phone of Susanna Sumner. I can't take your call right now, but do please leave me your name and number and I'll get back to you as soon as I can. Thank you.

The phone beeps, and I leave a message.

"Susie, I'm worried. You called me a couple of times, but I never heard you say anything. I text you and you don't respond. I call you, and you don't respond. You need to call me as soon as you get this message and let me know you're okay. Okay?"

I want to say more. Tell her I care about her and I'm worried. But I don't say anything like that, because I'm feeling like a chicken.

Instead, I end the call and set my phone on the couch, pissed at my bum knee, at the fact that I don't know where Susanna is and I have no other way to get a hold of her, unless it's through her phone. I don't know her parents' number or her brother's number, or even her best friend's number.

And that sucks.

The day drags, and still no response from Susanna. The sun goes down, it's almost six, and when my phone finally rings and I see Susanna's number on the screen, the relief that fills me almost makes my head spin.

"Thank Christ you're finally calling," I answer. "Are you all right?"

"Um, hello?" The timid voice that fills my ear definitely isn't Susanna's.

"Who is this?"

"Are you the sexy footballer?"

What the hell? "Who are you?" I ask.

"Um, my name is Claire Williams, and I'm a nurse. Susanna asked me to call the sexy footballer and let him know that she's going to be fine." She hesitates. "You are the sexy footballer, right?"

"Wait a minute." I sit up straighter, wincing at the pain shooting through my knee. "You're a nurse? And you're with Susanna?"

"Yes, she's in hospital, but don't worry, the accident wasn't that bad."

Fear makes my blood run ice cold. "Accident?"

"Oh dear, I'm sure you don't know, and I'm sorry to have to tell you like this. I'm afraid Susanna has been in a car accident, but she and her friend are okay."

"Her friend?" Who was she traveling with? That girl, Evie?

"Yes, I believe she was in the Mercedes with a man."

A man? "She wrecked the family Mercedes?"

"I wouldn't call it the family Mercedes. More like a sporty car. Two door. I heard it got mangled," the nurse says.

This conversation is confusing—and disconcerting. I can't believe the woman is calling to reassure me, yet she doesn't know shit. "So you're telling me Susanna was in an accident involving a two-door sporty Mercedes and she was with another man." Jealousy could be coming at me fast and hard right about now, but I can't even think about that. Not without knowing exactly how Susanna is.

"Er, some of my facts might be wrong. I'll have her ring you as soon as she's lucid. I only made this call because she kept babbling about her sexy footballer and how your number was under that exact term in her contacts and so...I had to help her and see for myself. You'll hear from her soon!"

There's a click, and then she's gone.

"Fuck," I mutter, dropping the phone beside me on the couch and scrubbing my face with my hands, my mind spinning. The nurse didn't tell me shit, beyond a bunch of garbled facts that might not even be facts.

Where is Susanna? Is she okay? What exactly happened to her? Is she badly injured? I can't sit here not knowing, but having her clear across the world kind of stifles my plan of action. Worse, I'm not even home. I'm stuck in a hotel in Arizona.

Grabbing my phone, I go to my favorites list and hit Tuttle's number.

"Hey, man," I tell him when he answers. "I need your help."

An hour later and Tuttle and our friend and teammate Tucker McCloud are at my hotel room, bringing a box of pizza with them and all the information about Susanna I need from Tuttle. How he finds this stuff out, I don't know, but I don't ask too many questions.

Let's just say Tuttle has excellent resources, and they all come from his father's business—and money.

"She's at County Hospital, just outside of Durham," he tells me as I stuff my face full with actual, real pizza. None of that thin British crap from PizzaExpress. "Don't know the extent of her injuries, though. Has she called you back yet?"

"No," I say after I swallow. Damn, I wish I could have a beer, but I'm on pain meds and I'm not mixing them with alcohol. I need to keep my head clear. "I wish she would. It's killing me, thinking that she's hurt and I'm so far away."

"You all right, man? I know this has gotta be hard on you." Tucker watches me, a sympathetic look in his eyes. He's a little older than us, he's bounced around from team to team throughout his career, and he's glad to have found a home with the Niners. He gives good advice, he gives us endless shit, and he's a solid friend.

"Yeah, I'm doing okay." Not really, and I think Tucker can tell I'm lying, but I don't know what else to say.

And I sound like a real wimp if I start whining too much about Susanna. But shit, I'm worried. I want to know where she's at.

I want to make sure she's all right.

"So tell me what else you've found out," I say to Tuttle.

"I found the phone number for her best friend, Evie. And I think I found her brother George." Tuttle taps away at his phone and mine dings, indicating I received a text message. "I just sent both numbers to you."

"Think I should call them?"

Tucker's nodding as Tuttle says, "Shoot them each a text first. See if they're who you're looking for. It's late over there now, so they might not respond." He shakes his head. "Sorry about this. I don't know what I'd do if I were in your shoes."

I grab another piece of pizza and chomp into it. Despite my worry, I'm also starving, and I can't concentrate when I'm so damn hungry. "You really don't know what you'd do?"

"Well, I have an idea of what I might do," Jordan says.

"And what's that?"

"Go to her," Tucker answers first. "Tell her how you feel. Take care of her as best you can, even though you're a little broken yourself."

"Yep. That," Tuttle agrees, tapping his fingers on the small round table we're sitting at. "If it was Amanda, I'd probably buy a one-way ticket to London, and the minute I landed I'd get a rental car and drive straight to that hospital. Make sure she's all right. I wouldn't sleep at all until I had confirmation."

I swallow the last bite of my slice of pizza and wipe my mouth with a napkin. "See, I was thinking of doing exactly that, but figured I was overreacting."

"You're only overreacting if you don't give a shit about this woman." Jordan watches me for a second, a knowing gleam in his eye. "But I get the idea that you actually *do* give a shit about her."

"I think I'm in love with her." My voice is gruff with the admission and I clear my throat, surprised at how easy that was to say. I haven't seen her in well over a month, and the last time I talked to her, I lied to her, which is absolute bull-shit and I feel like a total jerk. But yeah.

I'm pretty sure I'm in love with her. She's all I can think about. It's all I do—think about her. Football may consume me, but something else consumes me now too.

And that's Susanna.

Forgetting all about the pizza, I grab my phone and open the airline app I always use, entering info for a one-way ticket to London. After a few seconds I've got hits. "There's a connecting flight leaving in a little over three hours."

"That's great, but you need to make a few calls to your bosses first, before you leave," Tuttle reminds me. "You can't just bail, even though you're not playing tomorrow."

"They'll be a little pissed if you leave the *country* without letting them know," Tucker adds sarcastically, making me pause.

Damn, yeah. They'll want to get me in to see a specialist first thing Monday to check out my knee. Then they'll probably start scheduling physical therapy appointments and all that bullshit. Prep me for the press release and schedule a few interviews so I can talk about it to the press—the very last thing I want to do.

But there's no way I can stay. I need to go find Susanna. "All right, I'll put in a few calls, make my arrangements, and get the hell out of here."

"You got your passport?" Tucker asks.

"Never leave home without it." Thank Christ I got into that particular habit.

"You're golden then," Jordan says, smiling at me as he rises, giving me a slap on the back as he walks past, Tucker following behind him. "Let me know if there's anything else we can do."

"You guys have done more than enough," I tell them as they head for the door. "Thanks for the pizza. And the information."

"You know we've always got your back, Cannon," Jordan says. "No matter what."

"Yeah." I smile at them both. "I do."

TWENTY-SIX

SUSANNA

EVERY SINGLE BONE in my body *hurts*.

Wait, maybe it's my muscles that are causing so much pain. I'm not sure. All I do know is that I ache. Everywhere. My head. My neck. My shoulders.

My everything.

The nurse who was standing by my bedside when I woke up earlier in the morning informed me I have a broken arm and a couple of dislocated ribs. Some bruising on my face. Otherwise, I'll be fine.

I don't feel fine, though. I feel like that Mercedes actually ran over me.

A groan escapes at the thought of the car I was driving last night. Evie's car.

Now destroyed.

Shit.

I don't remember a lot of what happened last night after we left my parents' house. The rain was coming down in sheets. The road was slick, it was so bloody dark, and my glasses didn't seem to help whatsoever. No streetlights that far out in the country. I was driving an unfamiliar car, and that thing has the most powerful engine ever. I barely touched the gas with my foot and the car would leap forward like it was an impatient dog tugging at its leash while on a walk through a new neighborhood.

Priscilla expressed her worry a few times during the drive, but I reassured her I knew what I was doing.

Did I really know?

Apparently, no. One minute I was driving along the bendy country road, the next the car was spinning out of control until it landed on its side in a ditch. Thank God the ambulance came quickly, loading the both of us into it, but Priscilla barely had a scrape. I'm the one who took the brunt of it.

And now here I lay in a hospital room, in absolute agony, and I'm terrified my best friend is going to storm into my room at any minute and chew me out for destroying her beloved car.

Not that Evie would actually do that, but you never know...

A nurse enters the room, her steps whisper-quiet thanks to the shoes she's wearing. "Good afternoon. Looks like you're finally awake."

"It's the afternoon?" My voice sounds like I swallowed gravel.

God, did I?

I could've.

"Yes, you've been sleeping for quite a while, but they gave you a sedative, so no surprise." She has a clipboard in her hands and she ticks off a few items with a flick of her pen. "How are you feeling?"

"Like I ran over my body with a car," I complain, making her smile.

"I see your friend didn't stay overnight, so he must be all right," the nurse continues.

"He?" She couldn't have mistaken Priscilla for a man, could she have? No. Priscilla is tall, but she has long hair and she's beautiful.

"Well, yes, you arrived last night because of that car accident, right? And there was a man in the car with you?" She's frowning, waiting for me to answer.

"I was driving my friend *Priscilla* home. Though you really can't call us friends, since we only just met yesterday. You see, she's my brother's girlfriend, but it turns out she really wasn't his girlfriend at all, and my brother is actually in love with my best friend—"

"I must've been wrong then, that you came with a man. It was rather confusing last night, lots of accidents because of the terrible weather," the nurse says, interrupting me. "I'm glad to see you're in better spirits. They might even release you later today, though I'm not sure. Do you have someone who can come pick you up?"

"Yes. No. I don't know." I pray they don't release me to my parents. Unfortunately, their house is closer than my flat in the city, so that makes the most sense. And I have no clue where George or Evie are.

All I know is, I don't want to be held captive in my childhood home with broken bones and limited mobility. That sounds like absolute torture.

"Did you ever get a chance to talk with your footballer?" the nurse asks as she bustles around my room, checking all the things.

Wait a minute. "What do you mean?"

The nurse pauses in what she's doing. "Your sexy footballer you had me call last night. You wanted me to let him know you were all right."

"I did?" I don't remember this.

"Yes, you told me you had his number saved under Sexy Footballer, and you begged me to call him. Said you'd been trying to ring him all night, but he wouldn't answer," she continues, sounding so very matter-of-fact.

All the while my head feels like it might spin right off my body.

Cannon. I need to call Cannon and tell him what happened to me. Is he worried? Has he tried to call?

God, I feel terrible.

"I must call him," I tell her as I try to sit up. All that does, though, is hurt my head, my ribs, all of it, and I lean back into my pillow and close my eyes, hating how weak I feel.

"You can call him later. Perhaps when you return home?" The nurse leaves before I can answer her, and a frustrated sound escapes me.

I have no idea where my phone is, though they'd probably tell me I can't use it. I have no idea where my family is either, or my friend. I'm all alone in this hospital bed, and I'm groggy from the sedative and sore...

"There's our girl!" Father exclaims as he enters my hospital room, Mother right behind him. "We've been waiting all day to see you."

"All day?" I'm frowning.

"We've been in the waiting room worried sick about you." That's actual, genuine concern in my mother's voice as she rushes toward my hospital bed and carefully takes my hand. "Are you all right?" She brushes the hair away from my forehead and I flinch, surprised that even that tender action hurts.

I'm also flinching because my mother is actually being so...sweet.

Maybe something's wrong with her.

"I ache everywhere," I confess, surprised to see the sympathetic look on her face. "Especially my ribs."

"You dislocated a few," Dad says. "How's the arm?"

I glance down at my right arm in a black sling. "It hurts a little."

"The nurse told us they're going to cast it first thing tomorrow," Dad says. "Bright neon pink if you want it!"

He's talking like I'm ten, and I almost roll my eyes, but then I see the concern in his gaze, the weariness in the lines in his face, and I realize I've worried them both.

And for some reason, the realization makes me want to cry.

Tears suddenly streaming down my face, I tell him, "I want out of here."

"Ah, darling, don't cry." Mother tries her best to enfold me in her arms, but she bumps against my broken arm, making me cry out in pain, and my ribs are killing me. She finally gives up and pats me on the head like I'm an obedient dog. "The doctor said he thinks you should stay another night. They want to monitor those ribs. Make sure you don't have any internal bleeding."

Internal bleeding? That sounds serious.

"You're not currently bleeding internally," Father adds as he paces the length of the room. "They just want to make sure."

"Okay," I say weakly, glancing down at my arm. Maybe I do want a neon-pink cast. I wonder if Cannon would sign it...

Cannon probably won't even be able to see me wearing it.

"Where's Evie and George?" I ask, noting how Mother's lips thin, but otherwise she doesn't react to those two names said together.

"They're somewhere in the hospital," Dad says, pausing mid-pace. "I think they went to the cafeteria."

My mind automatically wonders if Evie is trolling for handsome doctors, but then I remember she's in love with my brother, so I keep that thought to myself. "Is she mad at me for wrecking her car?"

"Mad at you? Of course not," Mother says with a firm shake of her head. "She was so worried about you. And Priscilla too."

"Priscilla is fine, by the way. They didn't even keep her overnight. I believe she just got a few bumps and scrapes. Though you already know this," Father says to me—or to my mother? I'm not quite sure.

Mother says nothing, just shoots my father an irritated look.

"We made George call to check up on her," Father tells me with a little smile.

Well, that conversation must've been awkward.

My parents continue talking, but I'm not really listening, and I don't think they expect me to. I'm so drowsy, and finally I give in, closing my eyes as I try to focus on their droning voices. They talk for what seems like hours, the sounds merging into each other until I can't decipher what they're saying. At one point, I swear I hear other voices— possibly George and Evie have entered the room—but I'm too tired, and my eyelids refuse to lift to see what's going on.

Instead, I drift off to sleep.

And dream of Cannon coming to see me in my room. He walks in with a giant bouquet, so big and tall I can't see his face at first, and when he sets the bouquet on a nearby table, I burst into tears at seeing him.

He says those sweet, sexy, vaguely inappropriate words like he does, and I get embarrassed because my parents are still in the room, but I don't care because he surprises me with a giant diamond ring dangling from his pinky and then he's slipping it on my ring finger, declaring his eternal love for me in front of my family.

I've never felt more alive, or more loved.

So the disappointment is extra sharp when I open my eyes hours later to realize I'm alone in my dark hospital room, no massive bouquets waiting for me, no diamond ring glittering on my finger. Clearly the accident has made me delusional.

Clearly.

TWENTY-SEVEN

CANNON

I'M bone tired and operating on only a few hours of sleep, and my knee hurts like a bitch. If any of my coaches saw me right now, they'd probably tear me to shreds for walking through this hospital like a man hell-bent on finding the woman of his dreams.

Because that's who Susanna is. She's the woman of my dreams. The woman I know I love. Who cares if we barely know each other? Who cares if we've only spent a few days together? Those were the most magical days of my life, and when you know...well.

You know.

And I know without a doubt that I love Lady Susanna Sumner.

"Sir! Sir!" A receptionist is yelling at me as I walk past a check-in desk, trying to get me to stop, and I do, because I'm hoping she'll help me.

"I need to find a patient," I tell her as I set the bouquet of red roses I got for Susanna in the gift shop on the high counter.

She gazes up at me, her eyes wide, her lips parted. I'm probably scaring her. I'm sure I look like hell. I haven't shaved in days, I've been wearing the same clothes for the last thirty-six hours, and my hair is a mess. I bet I smell too.

Great.

"What's the patient's name?" she asks, fingers poised over the computer keyboard in front of her.

"Susanna Sumner."

The woman types in Susanna's name, then grabs her mouse and clicks. Then clicks again. She's chewing on her lower lip, her eyes scanning the screen before her until she finally looks up and meets my gaze. "Sir, I'm afraid it's too early for visiting hours."

"You gotta be kidding me." I glance around, my gaze setting on the plaque nearby that has the visiting hours listed. I check my phone.

Yep. I'm too early.

"It looks to me that Miss Sumner is being released this morning. Are you picking her up?" She tilts her head to the side, and I think she's trying to tell me something.

"Yes," I say slowly, and she nods, encouraging me to keep talking. "I'm picking her up, and taking her home."

"Perfect. She's in Room 204." She smiles, but I'm already gone, the vase of roses clutched in my arms, headed down the hallway as fast as my bum knee will take me.

I come to a stop in front of the partially open door and peer inside, but I only see the foot of her bed. Looks like no one else is there, and I'm relieved. I want to her meet her family, but not yet.

I want her all to myself for a little bit first.

Quietly I creep into the room, coming to a complete stop when I see my angel lying in bed. She looks...terrible. There's a gash across her forehead, her left eye is bruised, a horrific combination of purple and yellow, and her left arm is covered in a hideous neon-pink cast. The hospital bed is propped up and she's lying there with her eyes closed, her chest slowly rising and falling.

But I see her beneath the wounds and she's still beautiful. Of course, she is. Seeing her hurt like this reminds me that she's also incredibly fragile. Something worse could've happened to her, something traumatic, life-changing. And I don't know what I would've done if that was the case...

"Cannon," a voice breathes. "You're actually here."

Her eyes have popped open and she's staring at me, like I'm an apparition she dreamed up. I approach her bed, scared to touch her, yet desperate to touch her too.

"I'm here." I smile at her. "You okay?"

"Why aren't you at home playing your game?"

I frown. "I can't. I hurt my knee, remember? Besides, it's Monday. The game's over." And damn it, we lost.

"Oh." She's frowning too, glancing down at her arm in the pink cast. "That's right. I don't know how I forgot."

"You've been a little preoccupied," I tease, setting the vase on the table closest to her. "I brought you flowers."

"Just like my dream." She smiles, she's not making much sense, but I'm rolling with it. She's probably hopped up on meds. Hopefully only mild painkillers, though. "I thought you were still in my dream when I first saw you."

"Nah, I'm here. Hopped the first plane I could find to get to you." I shove my hands into the pockets of my jogger sweatpants, feeling awkward.

Cautiously, she scoots over on the mattress, patting the empty spot beside her. "Come here."

"Are you sure?"

"Please." Her expression is serious. "I want to touch you. Make sure you're real."

I go to her bed and perch myself on the edge of the mattress, careful not to bump into her. Being this close, I can really see the damage the accident did to her. There are little scratches all over her face and neck, a strangely shaped bruise across her collarbone that I'm thinking the seatbelt might've caused.

Reaching out, I tentatively touch her hair, pushing it away from her forehead. "My poor baby," I murmur.

She smiles and closes her eyes, a shuddering breath escaping her. "I'm so glad you're here. Next to me."

"You have a black eye." Leave it up to me to state to the obvious.

"I know, I'm sure I look awful. I feel much better, though. At least my body doesn't ache everywhere anymore," she says, her eyes sliding open. "Maybe you should kiss me," she whispers.

Thank Christ the airline provided me with toothpaste and a toothbrush before I got off the plane. Leaning in, I gently kiss her lips, not wanting to touch her anywhere else.

"You really are here," she says, her voice soft, her eyes dancing with happiness. "No one makes me tingle with just a kiss like you do, Cannon Whittaker."

I smile, readjust my position, and grimace with pain. She spots it immediately. "Is it your knee?"

"Yeah," I grit out, rising back to my feet. "I can't sit like that for too long. Hurts too damn much."

"Oh, Cannon." Her face falls. "I feel terrible. I'm so sorry."

"Not your fault." I shake my head. "It's worse than I told you. I need surgery. I can't play the rest of the season. This injury could—end my career."

"Oh no, I don't believe that. You're too strong to have a knee injury put you out of football forever." Her firm voice, the determination I hear there, the absolute belief in me, makes my heart, my entire body relax. I didn't realize I was so damn tense.

Just seeing her, hearing her voice, is making me feel better.

"We'll see," I tell her, but the doubt isn't as strong anymore, and I'm pretty sure I owe that all to her.

She contemplates me, her gaze dropping to the brace wrapped around my knee. "You flew all the way to England to see me? With your knee like that? When you need surgery?"

I nod. "Sure as hell did. Had to make sure you were all right."

"I'm guessing you're skipping doctor's appointments to do this?" She raises her brows, dropping them immediately with a wince.

Bet that hurt.

"Maybe." I shrug. "I can go see the doctors when I get back home."

"And when will that be?"

"Not sure. How long do you need me to stay?"

She looks ready to burst, she's so happy at my words. "However long you can."

I'm hoping a week. It might be less. Then again, it might be more. Even better, maybe I can convince her to come back with me for a little while.

"Is someone coming to pick you up?" I ask.

Susanna makes a little face. "My parents. They'll probably be here any minute."

"I get to meet the dragon lady?" She told me a few choice things about her mother, and how her friend Evie gave her that nickname. She also told me how hard she is on Susanna, which I don't particularly like.

"Actually, she's been really sweet since I got into the accident. Nothing like a car crash to remind my mother that she needs to get over herself and her exacting standards," Susanna says sarcastically.

"I'm glad she's being nicer," I say, and I mean it. I don't know what I'd do if my mom and I didn't get along, though she's all I got, and I'm all she has. We have to be nice to each other or else we're all alone in this world, with no real family to anchor us.

"I have so much to tell you." Susanna's entire face lights up. "I went to my parents' house on Saturday with Evie and so many *things* happened."

"Tell me about them later, okay? Don't overexert yourself. We need to get you out of here first." I walk around her room, looking for her belongings, opening a slim door that looks like a closet to find her purse and a small duffel bag sitting inside on the floor. "Is this your stuff?" I call from the closet.

"Probably. Oh." Her voice changes, becomes a little higher. "Father. Mother. You've made it."

I whip around to see her father walk in, a tall, thin blonde woman following behind him. They don't even notice me, they're too focused on their daughter lying in that hospital bed, and I can't blame them.

She's become important to me in such a short amount of time, she's all I can focus on too.

Grabbing her things out of the closet, I shut the door and then turn back around to face them. Her father notices me first, coming to an abrupt stop when his gaze lands on me. "Oh. Your fellow is here, Susanna."

Another man who states the obvious.

"I had to make sure she's all right," I say as I approach him, thrusting my hand out for a shake. "It's good to see you again, my lord."

"Please. Enough with the *my lord*," her father says, giving my hand a firm shake. "Call me Harwood."

I chance a look over at Susanna. From the pleased expression on her face, it appears I've just made progress. But her father's not the one I worry about.

It's her mother.

"Hello," she says coolly, taking the initiative first. "You must be Cannon."

"I am." I'm at a loss. Should I try to shake her hand too, or is that a no-no?

"It's so very nice to meet you." She offers her hand and I guess it's not a no-no, so I shake it.

"Nice to meet you too," I say warily.

She takes a step back, crossing her arms as she contemplates me. "You must really care about our Susanna if you jumped on a plane and flew all the way here to check on her wellbeing."

"When I heard she was in a car accident, I had to come and make sure she was okay," I say.

"Don't you have a football game to play?" her mother asks.

I point at the brace on my knee. "Hurt myself during practice and got pulled from the game."

"Oh, I'm so sorry to hear that." She actually sounds sorry too. "Are you all right?"

"My season is over. I'll have to have surgery."

All three of them make the proper sympathetic noises, not that I'm here for their sympathy. I want to focus on Susanna.

"She's getting checked out today, right?" I ask her parents.

"I just spoke with the nurse, and she said the doctor should be here soon to sign the release papers. Then she'll be free to go," Harwood explains.

"We'll be bringing her back to our home," her mother says. "You're more than welcome to join us."

"Mother," Susanna says, causing all of us to turn our attention to her. "Now that Cannon is here, I'd rather go back to my flat."

Mom and Dad are hardcore frowning. They don't like this idea one bit.

"Are you sure, Susanna?" her mother asks. "Won't you need assistance? You have a broken arm."

Susanna nods, her gaze locking with mine. "I'm positive. I know Cannon will take proper care of me. And I'll learn to adjust with the arm. I'll be fine."

There are all sorts of things I want to respond to that declaration, and not a one of them is polite. Instead, I clamp my lips shut and nod, hoping I look like a capable enough human being that's able to take care of Susanna in her time of need.

"Very well then," her mother says with an irritated sigh. "Though if you need us, you can always call. We'll come right over and pick you up."

"Of course." Susanna's still looking at me, and the curve of her lips is downright irresistible. If we were alone, I'd be kissing her right now.

Maybe it's good we're not alone. I need to work on trying to control myself around her. She's hurt. I'm hurt. We do something crazy, and we're bound to get hurt even worse. I can't chance it.

Sounds like the next few days are going to be rough.

TWENTY-EIGHT

SUSANNA

THE MOMENT CANNON slides into the driver's seat of the huge Range Rover he rented for his stay and slams the door, I'm practically crowing with pleasure.

"Oh my gosh, you arrived in the nick of time, I swear!" Leaning over very carefully, I brush a kiss on his bristly cheek. He looks exhausted, yet he's the most handsome man I've ever seen, even when he's tired.

He turns his head, our lips connecting, and just like that we're kissing. For real. Our lips part and our tongues dance and my entire body is tingling. Yet all he's doing is kissing me, not touching me anywhere else. Just lips on lips. Tongue on tongue.

I don't ever want it to stop.

A horn honks and I realize we're congesting the pick-up/drop-off area in front of the hospital. "We should probably go," I murmur against Cannon's lips.

"It's a long drive back to London," he murmurs in return, kissing one corner of my mouth, then the other.

"I know," I say with a sigh. "But just think of what we can do when we get to my flat."

My words work like an invigorating slap of reality. He shifts away from me, puts the car in drive, and pulls out of the drive, frowning as he grips the steering wheel. "We're not doing anything like that for the next few days while you recover, Susie."

"Seriously?" I sound like a child who's wailing after her toy got taken away.

"I'm afraid I might hurt you. And my knee is all jacked up," he mutters, staring straight ahead, his eyes never straying from the road.

I cross my arms and slump in the seat as best I can, but that hurts my ribs tremendously so I eventually straighten out and drop my arms to my sides. God, I can't even pout correctly. "This is terrible."

"What's terrible?"

"Having you so close and not being able to do anything about it."

He laughs. "It's good for us. Forces us to get to know each other even better instead of always getting naked."

"Maybe I like getting naked."

"Oh, I love getting naked with you, Susie. But not right now, not with your ribs and your arm and all that." He waves a hand at me, indicating...all of me. "You're packed in bubble wrap right now. A delicate little flower, too fragile to touch."

"That is the most ridiculous thing I've ever heard," I tell him, reaching out to touch his bicep. It's rock hard and warm and oh my God, I've missed him tremendously.

"You gotta stop touching me," he says, sounding vaguely irritated.

"My hand is just on your arm," I say, letting go of him.

"Yeah, but it drives me out of my mind. And I'm trying to concentrate on the road and scared I might jump over to the other side. You Brits got it all ass backwards," he says through gritted teeth.

"Um, I'll have you know we were here first, and you Americans ran away from us, so you're the ones who drive on the wrong side of the road," I point out.

"Whatever." He shakes his head and I sock him on the arm, unable to resist. "Didn't I tell you not to touch me?"

"Am I really that much of a distraction?"

"Yeah, you are. First you'll touch my arm. Then you'll touch other body parts, and the next thing I know, you've got your hand in my pants and your fingers wrapped around my junk and that just won't work. I'll crash the car, you'll get into another accident and might hurt yourself even more. It'll be all my fault, and your parents will hate me forever," he explains.

Hmm. He really does have a point. "You might be right."

"I *know* I'm right. You should take a nap."

He did grab that hospital blanket for me before we left the room. It's not the coziest thing—it's kind of stiff, a little scratchy, but at least it's something to keep me warm. I tug it farther up so it covers my chest, and snuggle into my seat. "This car is comfortable."

"Nothing but the best for my girl," he says, making me smile.

I close my eyes, appreciating the smooth ride. My car may be a Mercedes, but it's old, and it's low to the ground, so I feel every bump and dip I drive over.

This Range Rover, though, is a luxury ride through and through.

"You sleepy, baby?" his deep voice asks me a few minutes later.

I nod. "Mmmhmm."

"Get some rest. You'll wake up and we'll be at your place in no time," he encourages, his voice sounding distant...

MY EYES slowly open to find Cannon hovering above me, reaching across my lap to undo the seatbelt. "Home sweet home," he says, his voice soft just before he dips his head and kisses me.

A girl could get used to treatment like this.

"I'd carry you up to your apartment, but with my knee, I can't." He makes an apologetic face. "I hope you can walk up."

"Of course I can." It'll be a slow go, but I've got this.

"I'll help you," he offers, and I smile and say I'll be fine, but really, I'll probably need whatever help he can give me.

I wasn't exaggerating with the slow go. Between both of our injuries and trying to carry our bags and the vase full of roses, we're kind of a mess. And I only live on the third floor.

But that's the third floor, which means three flights of stairs, so it's quite the journey.

"I should've got us a hotel room," Cannon grumbles when we finally make it to my door. The hallway is so narrow, he's practically pressed up against me, and I really hope none of my nosy neighbors pop out of their doorways and start asking questions.

Luckily enough, most everyone is away at work, so no one will disturb us when I finally get the door unlocked and we both stagger inside my dark flat. I go to the window that faces the street and crack open the blinds, then hobble into the tiny kitchen and light a candle to take away the dank, damp smell that permeates the place.

One of the many joys of living in an old building.

"Are you hungry?" he asks.

"Not particularly," I tell him as I wander into my bedroom and set my duffel bag on the edge of the unmade bed. I'm such a sloppy mess, and if I wasn't in so much pain, I'd be scrambling about, tossing clothes in the washing basket, shoving shoes in the tiny wardrobe and making my bed. I'd run into the bathroom and pick up the towels on the floor, take the bras that dangle over the shower rod down, and try my best to appear as if I have my shit together.

But I don't have my shit together. I'm a bit of a disaster sometimes, at least when it comes to housekeeping. When you're raised with servants who pick everything up for you, how do you ever learn to clean up after yourself?

I sound like a spoiled brat, but it's true.

"Hey."

I glance up to find Cannon literally filling my bedroom doorway. He's so tall, he has to hunker down to fit, his arms above his head, hands gripping the top edge of the door-frame. Goodness, he's large, and I've rubbed myself all over that large body multiple times.

Despite the injuries and the pain and the difficulty I have breathing, I'm tempted to jump on him and beg him to have his way with me.

"Yes?" I ask, clearing my throat.

"First of all, you shouldn't be cleaning up." He enters my bedroom, glancing around the messy room. "We'll fix this later," he says, returning his gaze to mine.

"Fine," I say with a sigh, dropping the edge of the quilt that covers my bed.

"Second, I'm starving, and you have no food in your kitchen beyond some condiments in the fridge and stale crackers in a cupboard."

I grimace. "I'm a terrible cook." As in, I don't do it. Ever. Stems from that same problem I have about cleaning. When you have cooks who prepare you delicious meals morning, noon and night, you don't need to learn how to work in a kitchen.

"Know of any restaurants who deliver?" he asks hopefully.

"Plenty," I tell him as I whip my phone out of my yoga pants' pocket and open up a delivery app I use before I hand it over to him. "Look through the menus and see what you want."

"Awesome." He's scrolling through my phone, pausing every once in a while, and I just stand there staring at him, still in disbelief over the fact that he's here. With me. In my home.

All mine. To keep forever and forever.

Well. I don't know about that last part.

"You hungry?" he asks me when I remain quiet.

"You already asked me that a few minutes ago, remember?" I smile at him.

"Oh yeah, that's right. When I'm starving like this, I can't concentrate well," he admits sheepishly. He taps a few buttons the screen and then hands my phone back over to me. "I ordered something. It'll be here in thirty. Think I can borrow your shower?"

I bite my lip. "It's probably a mess. I had a body scrub spill last week."

"Is that like an oil spill in the ocean?" he teases.

"Sort of," I offer with a shrug, not willing to explain that I spilled half the tub of body scrub and it's so thick, I gave up trying to clean it. "I'm just warning you. It's probably not going to be the tidiest shower in the world."

"I don't care. I just need to get this plane sweat off of me. As long as you have a bar of soap and a clean towel, I'm good," he declares.

"A bar of soap? How very primitive of you," I say primly.

"Damn, I love it when you sound all snotty like that." He swats my butt, making me squeal, and I glare at him as he exits my bedroom. "Come on, girlfriend. Let's get you settled on the couch so I can jump in the shower."

I love how he oh-so-casually called me girlfriend. And I love that he's wanting to take care of me. So I let him. He positions me on the couch just so, with a few pillows from my bed propping me up and my favorite cozy throw draped over my body. Despite my protests, he's turned on the heat and promises to pay the bill, so I give in. My parents give me a substantial allowance, but I'm still cheap when it comes to heat.

I blame it on growing up in a drafty house.

Cannon rummages around in the kitchen and brings me a cold bottle of water, though I'd rather have tea. But I don't trust his American ways to make me a proper cup, so I'll deal with that later.

He hands over the remote, asks me if I need anything else, and then he's locked away in my bathroom, running the shower so hot I swear the steam seeps from the rather large crack at the bottom of my bathroom door and fills my flat.

This is heaven, I think as I turn on the television and pull up the guide to see what I can watch. There's nothing good on —every show that's currently airing is complete rubbish—so I turn the TV off and grab my phone to see I have a couple of missed text messages from Evie.

I heard your American boyfriend showed up and took you home!

Answer me, woman, and tell me you're alive!

Hmm, seems an alien has invaded Evie's body. She's not one to use exclamation points. Says they're pointless and juvenile.

Deciding texting her would take too long, I call Evie instead.

"Where are you?" I ask the moment she answers the phone.

"At my place. Why? Do you want me to come over?" she asks eagerly.

"Absolutely not." Perhaps I was a little too vehement in my protests. "I'm too tired. And plus, Cannon is here."

"I'm dying to meet him. Please. Let us come over."

"Oh God, you're with George." I do not want to imagine them having sex or whatever, gross.

"No, I'm not with George. He's at work. I'm all alone at my flat, bored out of my mind." She pauses. "Maybe we could get together later. For dinner?"

"Not tonight, I'm afraid." I sigh, my ribs aching. "I'm still in too much pain."

"Of course, I completely understand."

"Evie, is your—is your dad terribly angry about the car?" I ask, my voice weak, my stomach twisted in knots. "I feel so bloody awful about wrecking it. I can't imagine how mad he must be, especially since he's always telling you to be careful."

"No, *you're* the one who's always telling me to be careful," she teases. But then her tone turns serious. "He wasn't angry, Susanna. He's just thankful nothing too terrible happened to you. Says he's been beside himself with worry over you, as well."

"Aww, your dad is always so sweet," I say, fighting the tears.

"On you. Me? He's constantly telling me I need to do something with my life," she grumbles.

"Did you tell him about George?"

"Not yet." She sounds nervous. "I'm afraid he'll hate the idea."

"My brother is quite the catch," I remind her. "Handsome. And he's the most loyal man you'll ever meet, despite that whole Priscilla fiasco."

"You don't need to remind me. I'm quite aware of George's many fine qualities." She hesitates, sighing before she forges on. "It's just I haven't done anything for myself, you know? I live off my parents' money and I don't work."

"Neither do I," I point out.

"You have the art gallery."

"I only work there part time."

"But at least you get paid to do it," she says.

True. It is an actual paying job. I use the money to feed myself, mostly. Keep up my coffee habit.

"I need to find a purpose, Susanna. I just can't be George's girlfriend. I need to be Evie, who does…whatever."

We end the call with promises of a dinner date between the four of us in the next few days. Yet her words linger, making me wonder.

Am I selling myself short by not becoming something? I don't want to be the girlfriend of whoever, or the daughter of whoever. And I definitely don't want to become the wife of blah blah and the mother of blah blah blah.

I want to be me. Susanna, who's great at...

What?

TWENTY-NINE

CANNON

"DO YOU THINK I'M INTERESTING?"

I tear my attention away from Susanna's crappy not-4K television screen to focus on her. "What did you just say?"

"I asked if you thought I was interesting." She tilts her head, contemplating me. "Or do you find me boring?"

"You are the least boring person I know." I give her foot, which is propped on a throw pillow in my lap, a firm squeeze. We're extra careful around my knee, around her ribs and broken arm, because we want to keep touching each other.

And I can't stop touching her. It's like I'm addicted.

She rolls her eyes. "You're just saying that because you want to get into my pants."

"Well, there is that, but that sort of action isn't going down for a few days." No matter how bad I want it to, my girl isn't ready. My knee can't handle much, but I can lie on a mattress and just let her ride me.

A broken arm and healing ribs won't let that happen.

"I find *you* very interesting," she says, holding up her hand, her index finger pointing right at me. "One, you're American." She's ticking off all of my so-called interesting traits with her fingers. "Two, you're a football player for the NFL. Three, you came from a single mother, and look at you now. She must be so incredibly proud of you. Four, you could have all the fame you want, but you're not interested in any of that."

"I am nothing special. I happen to be good at football. That's it," I say.

"Five, you're incredibly modest." She shakes her head, smiling. "You're unreal, Cannon Whittaker. Oh, and six, you have the best name for a football player ever."

"You're going to make me blush," I tease and she laughs.

We're cuddled up on her tiny couch, her legs carefully draped over mine, me sprawled as best I can despite the knee brace and the miniature size of her furniture. It's late in the afternoon, I'm fed, I turned off my phone and it's raining outside.

I wouldn't mind spending the next few days just like this.

"I don't think you're boring," I tell her, breaking the silence. "It seems you've lived a pretty full life, and you're only twenty-three."

She waves a dismissive hand. "I hate that I'm only twenty-three. It sounds so young, though everyone considers me an adult, which I am, so that makes sense. But I wish I were twenty-five. That's a good age. A respectable age. Not a wayward teen, but someone older. Responsible."

"You're very responsible, Susanna. Despite what you say." Her brain and the way she thinks is fascinating to me. "Don't rush yourself. Enjoy each year you're given," I tell her, sounding like an old man trying to offer up some wisdom. I'm only a couple years older than her, but sometimes she just talks so young.

"Okay, wise one," she teases, nudging my lap with her toes.

I grip them in my hand, tickling the backs of them and making her wiggle. "Better watch where you put that foot."

"Why, are you going to strip me naked and check if I'm wet?" she asks hopefully.

"Lady Susanna Sumner, did you just say something about being wet?" Damn, we can't talk about this kind of stuff. Not tonight, not for the next few days. I'll get too riled up and then can't do anything about it.

"I did." She bites her lip, the look incredibly sexy. I've noticed that her hair is even more curly than usual, and I figure my earlier suspicions are true. She straightens the shit out of her hair to make it sleek, but I like her curly look too. "Am I going to get in trouble?"

"You wish," I tell her, making her laugh. "We can't mess around like that, Susie. No matter how bad I want to, I'm not going to do it. I might hurt you. Or I might hurt myself."

She sighs. "You are such a gentleman."

"You make that sound like a bad thing."

"When I want you to ravish me, yet you resist like a noble duke, then it *is* a bad thing." When I send her a questioning look, she shrugs. "I've read too many historical romances over the years."

"You read romances?" I'm surprised. I figured she'd be the type to read classic novels like the shit they tried to force on us in high school.

"I do, but I haven't in a while. Guess I'm too busy living my own romance," she says with a tiny smile.

"I wish I could make this visit with you more romantic," I tell her, feeling bad.

"You're very romantic, getting me whatever I want when I ask for it. Giving me a foot rub when I don't ask for it, which is even more thoughtful. You're tending to my every need, and it's wonderful." Her gaze drops to my knee in its brace. "I wish I could help you."

"I'm fine." I'm really not. My knee is throbbing. But I won't tell her that.

"You should go home so you can see the doctors," she says, her voice soft. "I'm sure they're anxious for your return."

I wouldn't know, since I turned off my phone and can't see their text messages, voicemails and emails. I'm sure I've got all three from a variety of coaches. I'm also sure they're pissed as hell at me that I've run away to another country and made myself unreachable.

Too bad. I have other things on my mind. Like this woman I'm sitting with.

"Do you care if we have dinner with George and Evie Wednesday night?" she asks, gazing at her phone. "Evie just sent me a text asking."

"That sounds good. I should still be here."

"Great." She taps at her phone screen and I hear the whoosh sound that tells me she sent a reply. "I can't wait for you to meet my brother and best friend." She makes a face. "It's still so strange to me that they're together."

She already filled me in on all the details from their wild weekend at her family estate. "If their relationship works out, I think you got lucky. Not only is Evie your best friend, but she could end up also being your sister-in-law."

Susanna smiles brightly. "Wouldn't that be amazing?"

I give her ankle a squeeze. "See? It's not strange that your brother ended up with her. It's a good thing."

We remain quiet for a bit, and nerves swirl in my stomach as I try to come up with the right way to tell her that I'm in love with her. Do I just blurt it out? Give her a little speech? Whisper a few romantic words and hit her with the most important info right at the end?

I don't know how to do this. I haven't told a woman I love her in a long-ass time, and what we share feels different. Susanna isn't some girl I had a crush on in high school. And she isn't a girl I had a thing for in college either.

She's a beautiful, intelligent and complex woman. A woman who breezed into my life in the most unusual way and ended up changing it completely. I'm a different man with Susanna by my side. There's so much still to learn and do, but I know without a doubt that she's the woman for me.

I don't want to let her go, but how do I make her a permanent part of my life? How do I convince her to come home with me, when *this* is her home? There's no way I can live here. Not yet at least. I have a life and a career back in California, and despite the knee injury, it's not over.

I refuse to let it be over.

This means I gotta go back—and I wanna take Susanna with me.

Will she go willingly? Or will she end it because we live in two separate worlds?

See why I'm so fucking nervous?

"Cannon."

I hear Susanna call my name and I look over at her, noticing the confused expression on her face. "I've said your name three times. Are you all right?"

"Just thinking is all," I say with a shrug, hanging my head so I can stare at her pretty bare feet. I'm not a foot man. I don't have that kind of fetish. With Susanna, I'm more of a tits and ass man because damn, the girl has curves, but her feet are pretty too. She's got cute little toes painted a deep red, and her skin is pale. I give her ankle a squeeze before I slide my hand up, under the black yoga pants she's wearing, encountering prickly skin.

"I haven't shaved in a while," she says, her cheeks pink. "I wasn't expecting you, and I was just in hospital, so..."

"I don't mind." Makes her more real anyway, and I appreciate that. If we can't be real with each other, then we're doomed.

"I call it my winter fur," she says with a smile, and I laugh.

"Doesn't feel much like fur right now," I say, smoothing my hand up the length of her calf.

"It's in its growing-out stage." She's laughing too. "I've never let a man see my winter fur before."

"I'm getting a lot of your firsts." My hand is on her knee now, my arm tunneling up the leg of her pants, and I know I'm playing with fire. I shouldn't touch her like this. Next thing I know, I'll have my fingers between her legs and she'll be begging me to make her come.

My cock twitches at the thought.

"I like that," she admits softly. "I want to give you more firsts."

My heart constricts. Damn, this woman. I can't take it anymore.

I gotta say something.

THIRTY

SUSANNA

CANNON'S LOOKING at me strangely. His eyes are fixed, directly on my face, and his hand is gently gripping my knee, his thumb stroking back and forth, lulling me. Luckily enough I have no injuries below the waist, so I am enjoying his wandering hands pain-free.

Wish he would touch me in more sensitive places, but I don't think I'm going to get that lucky.

"Susanna." His voice is scratchy, and he clears his throat, his serious expression making my nerves kick up a notch. "There's something I need to tell you."

Oh God. This is it. He's going to let me down easy. Tell me how much he's enjoyed our time together, but our relationship has too many obstacles and it's impossible for us to overcome them all. I brace myself, my ribs aching, the tears threatening as I focus on his mouth and the words that tumble forth.

"I'm in love with you."

Wait.

What?

"What?" I say out loud.

He smiles. And that's when I notice. He looks terribly nervous. His eyes are practically pleading with me to agree with him, and the hand still clutched around my knee is shaky.

"I'm in love with you. I know we haven't known each other very long, and I'm probably moving way too fast for you, but I love you. I want to be with you, and I will do whatever it takes to convince you that we're good together." He sounds fierce, he sounds like a fighter, and I know just hearing him say those particular words, in that particular voice, that he would fight for me.

Always.

"We *are* good together," I start, but he cuts me off.

"So good together, it's unreal. You're all I think about. You asked me if I thought you were interesting? You're the most interesting person I know. I can't stand being apart from you, Susie. I know I'm real busy with football, and maybe I didn't show it as much as you needed to see, but I missed you so damn much these last six weeks we've been apart. If we'd met during the off season, I could've devoted more time to you, but we didn't."

"We would've never met during the off season," I remind him, my voice gentle. "You came here to play football. This means football brought you to me."

"True." He smiles, and it's a beautiful sight. He's a beautiful man. Big and burly and a little rough around the edges and all mine.

Mine, mine, mine.

"I'm in love with you too," I say, my voice just a whisper. His eyes darken the second the words leave me, and then he's coming closer, his mouth landing on mine, his hand falling away from my knee to reach up and cradle the side of my face.

"You don't know how much of a relief it is to hear you say that," he murmurs against my lips seconds later, the both of us breathless.

"I thought you were going to break up with me," I admit, and he chuckles.

"Never." He kisses me again, then pulls away. "I want you to come back to California with me."

I'm gaping at him. "What?"

"I'm serious. Move in with me. Live with me. After I have my knee surgery, when I'm better, we can travel around the country. I can show you the sights," he says eagerly.

"But...what will I do in California? When you're in good shape and playing football once again?" My mind is awhirl with all the possibilities.

"You can do whatever you want." He's grinning, his hand still on my face, and I lean into his palm, closing my eyes for a brief moment, overwhelmed by his love, his words, our future.

Together.

This move, this relationship with Cannon, could be the change I so desperately need. The catalyst to push me out of my rut, to allow me to be free and figure out who I really am.

I want to go. I want the adventure.

I want a life with Cannon.

"If you need time, I totally understand. You have responsibilities here," he tells me when I must take too long to answer him. "I'm probably moving too fast for you."

"Yes." I shake my head, and his entire mood deflates. I realize quick my wrong choice of words. "Wait, I mean no, you're not moving too fast for me. I would love to go to California with you."

Before I can say anything else, he's kissing me again, his lips drugging me, putting me under his spell. "I'll make an honest woman of you," he whispers after he breaks the kiss. "When I take you to California, I'll find the biggest diamond I can afford and put it on your finger so everyone knows your mine."

I like his *mine* talk. It's a little caveman, and a lot sexy. "I don't need a big diamond," I tell him, lifting my right hand so I can tunnel my fingers through his hair. "As long as I have you."

"I'm giving you a big diamond," he says with finality, and I suppose I'm not going to protest.

Secretly, I always did want a large diamond on my finger so I can show it off. What woman doesn't?

"I'll have to tell my parents right away," I say.

"Think they'll be mad at me?" he asks with a frown.

"They won't be pleased I'm leaving. They'll worry about me and think I'm too impulsive, but I don't care. They'll have to get used to it." Now I'm the one who's cupping the side of his face. "Not to put any pressure on you, but if you do put a ring on my finger, that'll ease their worry somewhat."

"If you're cool with it, that's my immediate plan," he says eagerly.

"I am so cool with that," I say with a laugh, pulling him back in for a kiss.

"Everything's going to change," he tells me minutes later, when we're still snuggled together on the couch, the TV show forgotten, and we're only focused on each other. "When you come to California with me."

"I know." I'm grinning. "I can't wait."

EPILOGUE

Susanna

SIX MONTHS later

"Hey, got your text. Are you okay?" Cannon comes to a complete stop in the doorway, his eyes going wide when he sees me. "What the hell?"

I'm lying in the middle of the California king bed, wearing absolutely nothing. No bra, no panties, no nothing.

I am completely naked in the middle of the afternoon and I sent Cannon a silly text saying I needed him to come back to our suite right away. We're staying at a fancy hotel on Pebble Beach—we came with some of Cannon's teammates —and he was out golfing with them, but I got bored.

And horny.

"Damn, woman, I gave up my golf game for you." He's already tearing off his polo shirt, his abs rippling with the movement, and my fingers itch to touch him. Stroke him, lick him, suck him, all of the things.

All of the many, *many* things he likes me to do to him.

"I hope I'm worth it," I say innocently, my mouth dropping open when he undoes his khakis and reveals the monster erection stretching the front of his dark blue boxer briefs. He kicks off his shoes, sheds his pants and underwear, and then he's just as naked as me.

"You are so worth it," he says, his tone menacing as he stands at the end of the bed. Not menacing in a bad way, more like menacing in an *I'm going to eat you up and you're going to scream for more* way.

"What are you waiting for then?" I arch a brow, a move I've been working on for months in the mirror when I put on makeup in the morning or do my hair. Or brush my teeth.

Okay, fine, I've been practicing the move endlessly, and I finally think I have it down.

He practically leaps on the bed, the mattress sagging beneath his weight. I have a flash of worry for a moment—he only just wrapped up physical therapy for his knee, and I don't want him hurting it again—but I quickly realize he's fine.

And he's currently got his lips wrapped around my nipple, sucking it deep into his mouth.

I slide my fingers into his hair and keep him there, arching into his mouth, closing my eyes as the delicious sensation of his lips and tongue on my flesh washes over me. This never gets old.

Spending time with Cannon, talking to him, laughing with him, having sex with him, it never, ever gets old.

And I never, ever want it to stop.

"So wet," he murmurs when he slips his fingers between my legs and they come away dripping. I've been in a state of perpetual horniness since we've arrived in Carmel two days ago. I want to do it constantly. I don't know if it's the sea air that's invigorating me or what, but I'm not complaining.

And neither is Cannon.

"All for you," I tell him, and his eyes flare with heat. I've become a little more comfortable with the dirty talk and I even toss out the occasional raunchy comment, but that's rare.

Baby steps is what I tell Cannon.

"Hmm, can't wait to take a taste." He grins, moving down my body, dropping kisses here and there. Just below my rib cage. On my stomach, his tongue dipping into my navel and making me squeal. A kiss on one hip, then the other. His big hands spreading my legs wider, his mouth on the inside of my knee, trailing up to the inside of my thigh. So close. So very, very close...

His fingers in my pubic hair, the pubic hair he barely lets me trim. He's a total fan of the bush, as he calls it, and will hardly let me manicure it.

Finally, his mouth is exactly where I want it. Delivering sweet kisses. Hot breath. Teasing tongue. Fingers slipping inside my body, one, two at a time. He wraps his lips around my clit, sucking it, tonguing it, and already I'm close. The orgasm just out of reach, Cannon's mouth and fingers drawing it closer.

Closer still.

"Oh." The word falls from my lips, a warning, and he knows all of my tells. He increases his pace, fingers pumping, tongue flicking, and me coming. Shivering and shaking with his name falling from my lips, my fingers clutched tight in his hair, pulling. Probably hurting him.

I don't care. Neither does he. Every time he goes down on me, he gives me such a toe-curling orgasm, I tend to lose control. He knows this, yet continues to go down on me anyway.

That's the risk he's prepared to take.

"Mmm." Once my orgasm as subsided, he's lying next to me, his mouth on mine, the salty taste of me still on his lips and tongue. I kiss him eagerly, overcome with need for him and within seconds he's on his back and I'm on top of him, reaching for the bedside table and grabbing the condom lying there in wait.

I planned this interlude right down to every last detail.

"I'm feeling lazy," he tells me as I scoot down and tear open the wrapper, rolling the condom onto his thick erection. It flexes in my hand and I wrap my fingers around the base, giving him a firm stroke. He chokes out a groan, making me smile. "You gonna ride me?"

"You want me to ride you?"

"Yeah." He watches as I climb back on top of him, strad-dling his hips, lowering myself onto his cock. "I wanna watch your tits bounce."

I should be appalled that he calls them tits, but his words don't bother me. He loves my tits. And my plump ass, as he calls it, and especially my juicy pink pussy. His crude talk is but one of many reasons why I love him.

And I do. I love him so fiercely that when I think about it too much, my throat starts to feel tight and my eyes begin to sting.

Bracing my hands on the wall that is his chest, I start to ride him. Going slow at first, sliding up and down his erection, both of us moaning in agony when he fills me to the abso-lute hilt. He's long and thick and I feel so full every time we do this, yet it's like I can't get enough. I want more.

When it comes to Cannon, I'm greedy.

He rests his hands on my hips, guiding me, encouraging me to move faster. I follow his lead, bouncing harder, sending him deeper, the friction between us sparking, firing us both up. His hands move from my hips to my breasts, and he squeezes and kneads them. Suddenly he sits up, his cock still inside me, his mouth on my neck, my chest, the valley of skin between my breasts.

I wrap my arms tight around his neck and hold him, pausing in our movements. His hands go to my butt, fingers playing with the spot where his cock is filling me and I whimper in his ear. Those busy fingers slide up my butt crack, and my inner walls pulse and clutch.

"You love that," he whispers with satisfaction.

"I love everything that you do to me," I say with total and complete honesty.

"You especially love it when I play with your ass."

I sink my teeth into his shoulder muscle and he hisses in a breath. "You like it when I play vampire with you."

"I do like it when you bite me," he admits, his hips shifting. I can tell he's getting impatient—he wants to continue where we left off—and so I start to move again. Loving how intimate this position is, wrapped around each other, our sweaty bodies clinging, the sunlight from the giant window nearby shining upon us. All my flaws on display.

He loves every one of my flaws. He doesn't even see them as flaws. He only sees me.

Me.

Our breathing increases, the slap of our damp-with-sweat skin filling the otherwise quiet room, and he goes tense beneath me, his tell that he's close. His fingers dig into the flesh at my hips, his mouth breaking away from mine to exhale roughly, a groan emitting from low in his throat just before the shudders begin. I hold him close, working my body up and down his cock, another orgasm washing over me. This one like quicksilver. There and gone, slipping away just as I grab hold of it.

"Wow," he whispers against my throat once we've settled down. He kisses me there, his mouth rising, running along my jaw. "You can interrupt my golf game any time."

"Are your friends mad you had to leave?" I stroke his back, reveling in his smooth, muscled skin.

"More like they were worried about you."

"Oh." I swallow hard, fighting the guilt. "Now I feel terrible."

"Ha, got you." He tickles my waist and I sock him in the arm, annoyed. "They were glad I left. I was winning."

"You're a good golf player?" He's never really talked about golf before. I had no idea he could even play until he asked me about going on this trip a month ago.

"I'm good at everything I do." He waggles his brows at me. "Don't you know that by now?"

"I do know that you're good at loving me." I touch his nose with my index finger, my gaze snagging on the giant diamond resting on my ring finger. He gave it to me on Valentine's Day, a cliché we both acknowledged, but we don't care.

Love is love. We don't need Valentine's Day to declare it, but it made the moment memorable.

"It's like I was born to do it," he tells me, his warm mouth moving against mine as he speaks.

I kiss him, our lips clinging, our breaths mingling. "You do it so well," I tell him.

And he does.

Interested in Tucker McCloud's story? Then check out Nothing Without You, part of the Kristen Proby Crossover Collection, available now!

From New York Times and USA Today bestselling author Monica Murphy...

Designing wedding cakes is Maisey Henderson's passion. She puts her heart and soul into every cake she makes, especially since she's such a believer in true love. But then Tucker McCloud rolls back into town, reminding her that love is a complete joke. The pro football player is the hottest thing to come out of Cunningham Falls—and the boy who broke Maisey's heart back in high school.

He claims he wants another chance. She says absolutely not. But Maisey's refusal is the ultimate challenge to Tucker. Life is a game, and Tucker's playing to win Maisey's heart—forever.

The Kristen Proby Crossover Collection features a new novel by Kristen Proby and six novellas by some of her favorite writers:

Kristen Proby – Soaring with Fallon

Sawyer Bennett – Wicked Force

KL Grayson – Crazy Imperfect Love

Laura Kaye – Worth Fighting For

Monica Murphy – Nothing Without You

Rachel Van Dyken – All Stars Fall

Samantha Young – Hold On

Read the first chapter of Nothing Without You now!

NOTHING WITHOUT YOU EXCERPT

CHAPTER ONE

"Tucker McCloud is back in town."

I nearly drop the cake pan I'm carrying over to the counter at my older sister's nonchalant statement. I set it down with a loud plop, glaring at Brooke.

She doesn't even bother lifting her head. She's too busy studying her phone screen, scrolling through Facebook.

It's a Sunday afternoon and for some reason, I was full of nervous energy, so I decided to mess around in the kitchen like I do and come up with new cake flavors. When I texted Brooke to come over, she didn't even hesitate.

"Are you serious right now?" I practically screech, then take a deep breath.

No biggie. No big deal. Nope, I don't care that Tucker's back in town. It's probably a rumor. It's happened before. The residents of Cunningham Falls are always eager to welcome back their hometown boy who made good. The first football player from our high school to ever sign with the NFL, he's a big deal around here.

Not to me, though. I'd rather pretend he never even existed.

"His sister posted a photo of him last night," Brooke says, her eyes still glued to her phone screen.

I walk over to where she's standing, ignoring my rapidly beating heart. When she still doesn't bother looking up, I thrust my hand between her face and her phone, snapping my fingers. She hates it when I do that. "Brooke."

Brooke's head snaps up, her brown eyes narrow. "What?"

"Show me the photo." My voice is surprisingly calm, considering how jittery I suddenly feel.

She goes to the search box, enters in Tucker's sister's name —Stella McCloud—and clicks on Stella's profile. "Looks like they had a family get-together over the weekend, and Tucker came home for it," she explains as she starts scrolling, looking for those photos. "Ah, here they are—"

I snatch the phone out of her hand before she can say anything else, earning an irritated, "hey!" for my efforts, but I ignore her. I'm too hell bent on finding the photo of Tucker.

Brooke's right, I realize as I start examining each and every photo—forty-eight in all. There was definitely a family get-together over the weekend for the McCloud clan, and let me tell you, their clan is a big one. They're one of the largest families in the area. Tucker has lots of siblings—six besides him—and he's smack dab in the middle. The middle child always craves attention. It's a known fact.

And Tucker was the biggest attention hog I knew. From his antics on the football field and on social media, I'm guessing that's still true.

I stop on a photo of the entire family gathered together, and I spot him immediately. Very back row, on the far right. Tall and imposing with those broad shoulders and the light brown hair and the laughing eyes. Ugh.

He's still ridiculously good looking.

It's *so* annoying.

The photos are endless, and I'm surprised to see every single McCloud sibling is there. Only three out of the six remain in town, including Stella, the youngest. She's a teacher at the local elementary school, and Wyatt, is the football coach at the high school in the next town over. Wyatt is considered one of the most appealing bachelors left in the area—thirty-four, still single, attractive and with a good job. Women call him the uncatchable catch.

Just like his stupid twin brother, Tucker.

My ex-boyfriend. My high school sweetheart. The boy who took me to all the big dances, who made out with me in the cab of his truck after every single game, who snuck through my window in the middle of the night so he could sleep with me, even for just an hour. The first boy to tell me he loved me. The boy who gave me my first orgasm. The boy who told me he couldn't breathe if he didn't have me in his life.

This is the same boy who got a football scholarship from a D-1 school and broke up with me, all in the same day. So excuse the above fact I just listed. He didn't take me to *all* the big dances. I didn't go to his senior prom, but neither did he.

Little consolation for how badly he destroyed me.

"He looks great, right?" Brooke says, her innocent question breaking through my nostalgic thoughts. "Actually, they all do. The McClouds are a good looking bunch."

I pause on a photo of the brothers, four in all. Hunter, Colton, Tucker and Wyatt, their arms around each other's shoulders, matching smiles on their faces. Yes, they're all attractive. Hunter and Colton are both married, and Hunter already has children. The twins are single and handsome, but only one McCloud makes my heart thump wildly and my breath catch.

And all I'm doing is looking at a photo of him on Facebook, for the love of God.

"He looks phony," I say as I hand the phone back to Brooke, the only insult I can come up with in my muddled by Tucker brain. It's starting to hit me that we're in the same state. We're in the same town. I could bump into him at any given moment and I wonder what I might do if that happened. Hug him?

Or punch him in the face?

"Phony?" Brooke actually snorts, something she normally doesn't do. My older sister has her shit together. She owns Brooke's Blooms, and she is the most popular florist in town. Oh, and she just so happens to be married to one of the hottest men alive, Brody Chabot. They are so in love, it's a little sickening.

Fine, I'm just jealous.

"Slick. Almost too perfect," I say, redefining my phony statement. "Look at his hair." He has amazing hair. Soft. He liked it when I ran my fingers through it. I'd be sitting on the couch and he'd rest his head in my lap, staring up at me with his beautiful blue eyes, practically begging me to stroke his hair. And I always would...

Brooke comes to stand beside me, peering over my shoulder. "At least he still has hair."

"Why wouldn't he?" I ask incredulously, wondering if I'd still find Tucker attractive even if he was bald. Probably. "He's not that old."

"There were a lot of guys at my ten year reunion who were already balding," Brooke points out. "You said the same thing about yours."

Tucker didn't even show up to Brooke's ten year reunion— they graduated in the same class. "What does that have to do with anything?"

"I don't know." She shrugs. "I'm trying not to focus on his extraordinarily good looking face."

Huh. Of course, this means I have to stare at his extraordinarily good looking face. And my sister's right. He's so freaking hot.

I hate him.

"And his body. I mean, did you see the endorsement he had with that one underwear line a couple years ago? We pretty much saw everything." I glance up at her just in time to see her wrinkle her nose. "Some things I didn't want to see, too."

"Like what?" I saw the photos from the underwear campaign. I might have a secret board on Pinterest where I can study them on rare occasion.

"Like the outline of his—" Brooke points down below. "Junk. Some things I don't want to know, Maise."

Now it's my turn to grimace. "Some things I don't really want to know either, Brooke. Like you have an idea of what Tucker's junk looks like."

"I definitely know his junk is nothing to sneeze at." Brooke bursts out laughing the second she says the words. "I can't believe we're having this conversation."

"You're the one who brought it up!" I'm tempted to go on my phone and look at those photos again. I'm friends with Stella too. We were close in school. We still occasionally get together for lunch or drinks, and we talk about everything and everyone with the exception of Tucker.

Stella knows he's off limits.

"You think he already went back to California?" I ask when Brooke hasn't said anything.

"Why? Hoping you'll run into him?" Brooke smiles, her eyes sparkling. She just got back from her honeymoon and she's so happy. Wedded bliss looks good on her. Looks good on her husband, too. Brody can't stop smiling either. It's so sweet to see them together.

Makes me a little bit envious. I wish I could find someone like Brody. It's hard, though, when I'm so busy making wedding cakes for all the other blissed out couples in town getting married.

Speaking of wedding cakes...

"I need to frost this thing," I say, grabbing the cake pan and setting it on the cooling rack. "And then I want you to give it a try."

"You should've invited Brody over to sample it."

"Um..." I hesitate, not wanting to offend. "He kind of makes me nervous," I say with a wince.

Brooke glances up, her expression surprised. "But why? He loves everything you make."

"I don't know." I shrug. "I want him to be honest with me."

"He's always honest."

"He likes everything I bake. Even the gross stuff."

Brooke laughs. "He's easy to please when it comes to sweets."

"Uh huh." My voice is dripping with sarcasm and I grab the bowl full of frosting I made earlier. It's just the base. I'm going to add a few things to it now to correspond with the cake. "You're honest. You tell me if what you just ate is total crap."

"Nothing you make is ever crap, and you know it," Brooke says with all that older sister authority she's so good at delivering. "Sometimes, you get a little—out there with your flavors, but that's always in good fun. You know what works for your business and you stick with it."

"You might not say that about the cake I'm going to serve you here in a bit." It's orange. As in, it's flavored with orange, the cake itself is bright orange, and the frosting is going to have a hint of orange flavor, as well as a pale orange color. Simple, right? But kind of daring, because no one hardly ever has an orange cake anymore. It's always lemon. Sometimes strawberry, though that can be terribly sweet.

Orange is from the seventies. Mom still fantasizes about some orange Bundt cake she ate when she was a kid at someone's birthday party. She wants to find the duplicate of that cake. So when I'm bored, I go in search of it, trying to recreate her memories of sunshine and summer—that's how she describes the taste of the cake. Later tonight, I'll bring Mom a slice.

If it's any good, that is.

"I'm not worried," Brooke says with all the assuredness in the world. I appreciate her total belief in me. I always have. We've always been super close. Only a year apart in school, we shared friends, though never boyfriends, thank goodness. That would just be too weird.

Tucker was in her class, and so was Brody. Brody and Tucker were friends, though they didn't necessarily hang out together. Brody pretty much kept to himself. Brooke explained everything to me right before they got married, confessing that his father was a total monster. So he distanced himself from everyone, including Brooke.

Yet look at them now.

Sighing happily, I reach for the tiny bottle of orange extract and twist off the cap, adding a couple of drops to the vanilla frosting. I have a small bowl full of orange zest I made earlier, and I grab a pinch, sprinkling it into the bowl. Then I grab a spoon and start stirring.

"Not using your mixer?" Brooke asks.

"This one is—delicate," I tell her, hoping she understands. "I have to get the flavors balanced just right. I'd rather do it by hand."

"The master at work." Brooke rises to her feet and starts to exit my kitchen, coming to a stop right beside me so she can press a quick kiss to my cheek. "I want a slice, but I have to go."

I pause in my stirring. "You didn't even get to taste it yet."

Brody just texted me, asking if I'd meet him for dinner, so I need to go home and take a shower. He mentioned he has a surprise for me." She smiles. "You should join us."

Frowning, I shake my head. "What if your surprise is his—penis wrapped in neon pink paper?"

Brooke laughs, covering her mouth with her hand. "Seriously, Brooke! We're meeting for *dinner*. In public. He's not going to present me his penis at the dinner table."

This conversation just took a weird and confusing turn. "You never know," I mumble, my cheeks hot. I don't want to go to dinner with them. Oh, I know they'll include me in their conversations and make it be about the three of us versus the two of them, but still. I'll feel like a third wheel. Witnessing their love is both beautiful yet pathetic.

As in, they make a beautiful couple. And they make me feel pathetic.

"You're being ridiculous." Another kiss on the cheek from my sister and then she's gone, the scent of her flowery perfume still lingering in the kitchen. "I'm going to text you later!" she calls as she opens the front door. "Convince you to come to dinner with us!"

"And be the tag along little sister during your romantic dinner where he gives you a surprise? No thanks," I mutter under my breath, ignoring how my arm aches. My date tonight is with my kitchen and this orange cake. That way I can be alone with my thoughts.

My Tucker McCloud-filled thoughts.

———

Read Nothing Without You now!

WANT A FREE BOOK? SIGN UP!

Dear Readers,

I hope you enjoyed **THINKING ABOUT YOU!** If you haven't already, please sign up for my newsletter so you can stay up to date on my latest book news. Plus, you'll get a **FREE** book by me, just for signing up! Click below:

Monica Murphy's Newsletter

Are you on Facebook? You should join my reader group! That's where you find out all the good book news FIRST! Click below to hang out with us:

Monica Murphy's Reader Group

ALSO BY MONICA MURPHY

Standalone

Things I Wanted To Say (but never did)

College Years

The Freshman

The Sophomore

The Junior

The Senior

Dating Series

Save The Date

Fake Date

Holidate

Hate to Date You

Rate A Date

Wedding Date

Blind Date

The Callahans

Close to Me

Falling For Her

Addicted To Him

Meant To Be

Making Her Mine

Forever Yours Series

You Promised Me Forever

Thinking About You

Nothing Without You

Damaged Hearts Series

Her Defiant Heart

His Wasted Heart

Damaged Hearts

Friends Series

Just Friends

More Than Friends

Forever

The Never Duet

Never Tear Us Apart

Never Let You Go

The Rules Series

Fair Game

In The Dark

Slow Play

Safe Bet

The Fowler Sisters Series

Owning Violet

Stealing Rose

Taming Lily

Reverie Series

His Reverie

Her Destiny

Billionaire Bachelors Club Series

Crave

Torn

Savor

Intoxicated

One Week Girlfriend Series

One Week Girlfriend

Second Chance Boyfriend

Three Broken Promises

Drew + Fable Forever

Four Years Later

Five Days Until You

A Drew + Fable Christmas

Standalone YA Titles

Daring The Bad Boy

Saving It

Pretty Dead Girls

ABOUT THE AUTHOR

Monica Murphy is a New York Times, USA Today and international bestselling author. Her books have been translated in almost a dozen languages and has sold over two million copies worldwide. Both a traditionally published and independently published author, she writes young adult and new adult romance, as well as contemporary romance and women's fiction. She's also known as USA Today bestselling author Karen Erickson.

f facebook.com/MonicaMurphyAuthor

O instagram.com/monicamurphyauthor

BB bookbub.com/profile/monica-murphy

g goodreads.com/monicamurphyauthor

a amazon.com/Monica-Murphy/e/BooAVPYIGG

P pinterest.com/msmonicamurphy

Made in the USA
Las Vegas, NV
27 July 2023

75312825R00173